MISTRESS
OF THE
SOLSTICE

Anna Kashina

Dragonwell Publishing

Copyright © 2013 by Anna Kashina

Cover art by Howard David Johnson
Design elements by Olga Karengina

Published by Dragonwell Publishing
(www.dragonwellpublishing.com)

ISBN 978-0-9838320-4-1

CONTENTS

Herbs of the magic brew, six and six,
Blend at my will into potent mix.
Six herbs of darkness, six herbs of light,
Grant me the power, grant me the sight.

Light herbs are easy—pick them and toss them:
Color of bluebell, chamomile blossom,
Freshness of catnip, honey of clover,
Fire of lychnis, rose-bay flower.

Herbs of the dark are heady and strong,
Pick them is silence, sing them no song.
Dark herbs that seal the brew's potent taste
Cannot be named, or your work is a waste.

On the night of the Solstice, Love is the rule
Granted to all who tastes the brew.
Great God Kupalo, bless our crops,
Save us from evil, lift our hopes.

We all are consumed by love, lust, and glee,
Save for the Mistress, who must remain free,
For if the seed of Love in her heart doth bloom,
Our land will fall to the powers of doom.

The power of Kupalo goeth forth into ages,
Yet rule of immortal doth carry its doom.
On the night of the Solstice, a hero of legend,
Cometh marked by an arrow through turmoil and gloom.

His guides are the creatures of magic and wisdom,
His strength is no weapon, but fire in his eyes.
He carrieth death for the rule of the kingdom,
He bringeth new life for the new sacrifice.

MARYA

I stood beside my father and watched the girl drown. She was a strong one. Her hands continued to reach out long after her face had disappeared from view. The splashing she made could have soaked a flock of wild geese to the bone. She wanted to live, but there was no escape from the waters of the Sacrifice Pool.

I looked at my father's handsome profile. His pale face, awash with moonlight, looked magnificent. The power of the Solstice enfolded him. It made me proud to be at his side, his daughter, his head priestess. He was the one who mattered. The only one.

The girl's struggle ceased. The rippling water of the lake stilled, glittering in the silvery light of the near-full moon. We watched the flicker of the glowing candles set in the flower wreaths as they floated downstream. A few of the wreaths had already sunk—bad luck for their owners, who would most likely die before the next Solstice. Maybe one of them belonged to the next Sacrifice Maiden?

I felt my father stir next to me, as he too peered into the amber depths of the lake.

"A fine sacrifice, Marya," he said. "You did well."

"Yes." I closed my eyes to feel the familiar calmness wash over me. I was detached. I didn't care.

I didn't even know her name.

My eyes still closed, I sensed my father throw off his cloak and stand naked, his arms open to the cool night breeze.

"Bring her to me, Marya," he whispered.

I stretched my thoughts, seeking out her body tangled in the weeds on the bottom of the lake, seeking the spark of life that still remained there, trapped, beating in terror against its dead shell like a caged bird. I reached for it, brought it out, and gave it to my father. I sensed the moment the two of them became one, her virginal powers filling him with such a force that the air around us crackled with the freshness of a thunderstorm.

He sighed, slowly returning to his senses. I kept my eyes shut until he found his cloak on the damp grass and wrapped it around his shoulders. I sensed his aura returning as he once again became himself. The Tzar. The immortal. The invincible.

The undead.

We could hear people singing in the main glade. The celebration was at its full. Soon they would be jumping over the bonfire. As the night reached its darkest, quietest hour, they would break into couples and wander off into the forest. "Searching for a fern flower" they called it. Fern has no flowers, of course. But searching for it made a good excuse for seeking the solitude of the woods. Besides, the blood of virginity spilled on the Solstice night glowed like a rare, exotic blossom of true passion. Those who found their fern flowers tonight were blessed by Kupalo.

I could hear the whisper of every leaf, every tree, and every flower in the forest. This was the night when the powers of Kupalo roamed freely in the world; this was the night when everyone's mind was clouded by Love.

Except mine. Love had no power over me. My mind was free.

One year later...

IVAN

The room smelled of dust and stale bread. It looked far smaller than it had last night. The woman—Ivan had never managed to catch her name—was scooping ashes out of the large stove. There was a squeaking in the corner, and as he watched the woman's soot-stained hands, a gray shadow darted across the floor past her skirt. She paid it no notice.

Ivan pulled his pack away from the wall and leaned on his elbow, enjoying the warmth of the morning sunlight creeping in through a dusty windowpane.

The man at the table raised his eyes from the mug and stared at Ivan.

"What is the chosen maid's name?" Ivan asked.

The man sighed. "I'm warning you one last time. Let it be. You're an outsider. You'll never understand."

Ivan held his gaze. "I'd like to try. If you would be kind enough to explain, old father."

The man's gaze was heavy, unblinking. It was hard to read his expression.

"We've had many heroes come to our kingdom. They never asked any questions. They knew exactly what was going on and what they needed to do. And yet, they all failed. Why do you think you'll get anywhere by asking questions?"

"Because," Ivan said, "I'm not like any of them."

The man took a big gulp from his mug and wiped the foam off with his sleeve. "You're either very good, lad, or very stupid."

Ivan waited. The pause was long this time, yet he knew the man would speak.

"Pyotr and Vassa have six daughters," the man said at

length. "It is an honor for one of them to be chosen. When else can a common girl get to carry the fate of the kingdom on her shoulders?"

"How exactly does it work?" Ivan asked carefully.

The man's bloodshot eyes looked glassy. At first Ivan thought it was from the drink. Then he saw a tear standing in the fold of the man's sunburnt skin.

"Our kingdom is small," the man said. "In six days you can ride all the way across. And yet over the years it has withstood the attacks of armies that rolled from East to West, burning all in their way."

Ivan nodded. People in the last two kingdoms he'd passed through were so wary of strangers that he'd had real trouble finding food and shelter.

"Do you know what makes our kingdom invincible?" The man leaned forward, his beady eyes staring directly into Ivan's. His breath was foul, but Ivan didn't turn away. He waited.

"Love," the man said hoarsely. He dropped his head and sat for a while, breathing heavily, as if this one word had spent all his energy.

"Love?"

The man lifted his head and looked at Ivan for another long moment. "Our Tzar, Kashchey. Kashchey the Immortal, that's what he likes to be called. But village folks sometimes call him—" the man leaned close, whispering in Ivan's ear.

"The Undead?" Ivan repeated. He had heard the name before, though no one had ever talked about it openly. "But why?"

"Hush, lad!" the man commanded. "Unless you want to be stripped naked and thrown out of this village!"

Ivan shook his head. None of this made sense. Yet, it unnerved him to see the large, boar-like man in front of him so disturbed.

"What's it to you?" the man asked. "Why do you care so much?"

Ivan sighed. It was hard to explain to a stranger, especially

5

one so absorbed in his own worries. "It is a debt I must pay. To a friend."

The man frowned. "Does this friend mean so much to you? Enough to meddle with the Damned?"

Ivan smiled and kept his silence.

"You must owe him a lot," the man said.

"I owe him my life."

A shrug. "Lives don't mean much. Not in our parts, anyhow."

Ivan held his gaze. "They do, to me."

The man's chin trembled. He clasped it with his hand. "You're still young. Twenty summers, at most."

"Twenty four." It hardly mattered.

"You couldn't possibly understand."

"Try me."

The man's cheek twitched. Ivan had an odd feeling he was holding back tears, but the impression dissipated as the villager slammed his meaty hand on the dirty table top. "Leave it be." He pushed away and rose heavily to his feet. "I expect you'll want to move on as soon as possible."

Ivan narrowed his eyes, watching the man's face, small beads of sweat that rolled down his temple to rest in the folds of skin under the eye. The man was afraid. Terrified.

After everything he'd learned in the last few villages, Ivan was not surprised. He wondered how anyone could maintain a pretense of a normal life under this kind of strain.

He nodded his response to the man's prompting gaze and scooped up his pack as he followed the man toward the door.

"Just remember," the man warned him. "The Mistress will be here tomorrow to pick up the girl. It is an ancient ritual. We want no meddling do-gooders to disturb it for us. If we find that you and your beast companion are still nosing around—"

Wolf. Ivan felt an unbidden pang of worry. He dismissed it. Wolf had always been good at taking care of himself. "Don't worry," he assured. "We won't."

"Don't cause any trouble," the man persisted. "Pyotr's family is going through a lot already. I just hope—we all hope—his daughter will do." His eyes wandered to the curtained alcove above the stove where, Ivan knew, the man's own daughter slept. His face spoke without words. *I hope it is Pyotr's daughter and not mine*, it said. *Not this year. Not ever.*

"Right." Ivan flipped his pack onto his shoulder.

The man stood still for a moment. He appeared to be thinking hard.

"You might want to talk to Gleb," he finally said. "The herb man in *Zabolotnoye*."

Ivan turned, careful not to show any emotion. "The village behind the swamp?"

"There is no swamp. Dried off a hundred years ago, grandmother used to tell. It's just a name."

"How do I get there?"

"Follow the path east. It's far from here—almost twenty *versts*. But, if you're lucky, if you stay out of Leshy's way, you'll be there tonight."

Wolf was waiting outside the outer village fence, lying in the long grass. His head lifted up as he saw Ivan, his muzzle rising as high as Ivan's waist. It had a rust-colored patch of dry blood smeared into the fur around his nose.

"You surely took a long time, boy," he growled as Ivan approached. "And, you look too pleased with yourself."

"He told me how to find Gleb!"

Wolf rubbed a paw against his nose, melting the stain into the rusted gray of his fur. It was hard to imagine that he was capable of human speech. It was even harder to imagine that this large gray beast had been alive long before Ivan's home kingdom had risen from a group of troubled villages and local tribes. Ancient history, as far as Ivan was concerned. Yet, in the past year, he had come to terms with these things.

"And?" Wolf prompted.

"And what?"

"Are you sure it's the same Gleb?"

Ivan hesitated. He'd been so glad to hear the name from the villager that the possibility that it might belong to somebody else had never crossed his mind.

"He said Gleb the Herb Man. It seemed likely at the time. And, there is only one way to find out for sure. He's only twenty versts from here, in a village called Zabolotnoye."

Wolf nodded. "Assuming that old Gleb had decided to move back to the Damned Kingdom in the first place, it would be just like him to find some god-forsaken village for a home. How did Gleb's name come up? You didn't *ask*, did you?"

Ivan shook his head. "You told me not to. And, I didn't think they would know, anyhow. The man just mentioned him."

Wolf fixed him with a stare. "'Just mentioned him', eh?'"

Ivan nodded.

"People never 'just mention' anything."

"Perhaps," Ivan suggested, "they do if you give them a chance."

Wolf bared his teeth. "Perhaps you'd do better to move your smart feet. Twenty *versts* is a long way."

The man who opened the door had thin white hair falling past his shoulders and a long straight beard. He eyed his visitors calmly, like a man not prone to surprise.

"Come in." The man's gaze was directed past Ivan's shoulder.

With a shock, Ivan realized the man spoke to Wolf. The gray beast silently brushed past Ivan and padded to a small floor mat spread near the stove. After a moment, Ivan followed him inside.

The dark, warm room smelled of herbs. In the light of a thick flat candle floating in a clay dish of water, Ivan could see bundle after dry bundle hanging from the invisible beams of the dark ceiling and tied onto clothes lines, tangled like spider webs, just above his head. It took some effort to navigate through the thicket of dry stems. Their thick, heady smells made his head swim.

The dry warmth of the stove beckoned after the damp chill outside.

"It has been a long time," Gleb the Herb Man said. He was still addressing the wolf, but then he turned to look at Ivan. His dark eyes held quiet curiosity.

It struck Ivan as strange. As far as he could tell, there was nothing in him that called for such curiosity—a young man with blue eyes and straw-colored hair, wearing simple peasant garb. The villages in all the kingdoms were full of men who fit this description. But in the past year of traveling with Wolf, Ivan had gotten used to many odd things. A thin old man who talked to Wolf with familiarity and eyed Ivan as a curious beast was by no means the strangest of them.

"It was damn hard to find you, old man," Wolf growled. "I would have given up on you if the boy here hadn't dragged the information out of an unsuspecting villager. Who would have thought that you'd forsake your promise and settle back in the Kingdom of the Damned?"

A spark flared in the old man's eyes. "The Kingdom of the Immortal, you mean. Or, as people here like to say—"

"...The Undead," Wolf finished. "We know. Spare us the witty talk."

"So." Gleb's eyes returned to Ivan. The intensity of his gaze was unnerving. "You found yourself another hero."

"Yes."

"A strange choice. Not what I would have expected."

"I think," Wolf said, "what you expected is what *everyone* expects."

"Can't you just give up?"

"You know I can't."

"*I* did." A strange mixture of feelings filled Gleb's voice. Restraint. Bitterness. Pain.

Wolf nodded. "It was a hard loss for me. But I found myself another herb man. And, he brought this boy back from the dead. Now, the three of us are in this together."

"Yes," Gleb said. "The three of *you*. Yet, you came back to

9

me. What do you want?"

Wolf shifted to turn his back closer to the fire. The flickers coming through the narrow slits in the stove door made his coat glow like amber.

"Give the boy some food," Wolf said. "He's always hungry."

Now that Wolf mentioned it, Ivan did become aware of the emptiness in his stomach. His last meal had been with his hosts in the previous village. A twenty-*verst* walk through Leshy's woods was a great distance to cover in one day.

Gleb chuckled. "You came all the way here for food?"

Wolf growled. "A bloody waste of time, if you ask me. But no. He wants information. He's a talker, too much so for his own good."

"What do you want to know?" Gleb asked, turning his full attention to Ivan.

"I want to see the Mistress." Ivan swallowed, unnerved by the man's direct gaze. "To talk to her."

Gleb got up, reached into the top of the stove, and pulled out a bundle wrapped in a cloth. He set it on a bench and carefully took the cloth off. It was a warm cabbage pie.

"It is her father you need to see, . . . ?"

"Ivan," Wolf supplied.

Gleb's eyes lit up with sudden interest. "Ivan." He broke off a piece of the pie and gestured for Ivan to help himself.

The pie was still warm, with eggs mixed into the moist cabbage filling. Ivan hadn't eaten one like it since he'd left home.

"Hasn't Wolf told you?" Gleb asked. "Her father's powers feed off virgins. Without those girls he would wither like a corpse. It is their love that keeps him whole."

"Love?" It was the second time Ivan had heard the word today. Mentioned in connection with a dark sacrifice, it sounded offensive.

Gleb sighed. "Kupalo," he said, "is the god of the crops. Of fertility. You do know that true fertility feeds on love, don't you, lad?"

Ivan felt his ears get hot. Luckily, the room was dark

enough to conceal his blush.

"Our Tzar Kashchey," Gleb continued, "has found a way to tap into the power of Kupalo. It was even more ingenious than finding a way to separate himself from his own death and hide it in the tip of a Needle. One virgin a year—not too big a price for having a powerful sorcerer protect your kingdom, eh?"

"What Needle?" Ivan asked.

Gleb threw a glance at Wolf.

"Go on," Wolf prompted. "Tell him."

"Why haven't you told him yourself, Wolf? Why look for me in the first place?"

"We could have gone on without you," Wolf answered. "But no one knows more about the Solstice than you do."

"What about your other herb man?"

"He left this kingdom—too long ago. He already told the boy what he could."

"I see."

The pause seemed to last forever. The old man's slender fingers broke off pieces of the pie one by one. He chewed slowly, his eyes staring unseeingly into the distance. Finally he finished his share and leaned back against the wall. He looked tired.

"I don't see how telling him anything would help," he said to Wolf. "The Mistress has no feelings. Talking to her wouldn't do a thing. As for Kashchey—how do you persuade a wolf to give up his meat?"

There was a growl from the mat by the stove.

"Sorry," Gleb said. "It was a figure of speech."

"I want to try," Ivan insisted. "It wouldn't be right if I didn't try. Tell me how I might do it, old father."

The herb man chuckled. "Old—yes. But your father I certainly am not."

"You could help me. If you would."

"Like I said, young man. You need to see Kashchey, not his daughter. At least Kashchey will kill you quickly. The girl—she'll just make you fall in love with her and send you on an impossible task. No one has ever carried out one of her tasks and lived to tell the tale."

Ivan leaned against the wall, staring at the shifting shadows by the fire.

"I won't fall in love with her," he said at length.

Gleb shrugged. "They all say that, boy. You're no different than the rest."

Ivan held his gaze. "She's his victim too. She hasn't been given any choice. And everything she must do—it's just so wrong. I thought—maybe I'd convince her to help."

In the silence that followed, Ivan watched Gleb's shoulders shake with silent laughter. He turned to Wolf, but the beast's face was impenetrable.

"This one is even worse than I thought, Wolf," the herb man said. "A romantic. How could a bloody romantic possibly accomplish anything at all?"

Wolf only growled on his mat by the fire, shifting to expose his other side to the heat.

Ivan sat up straight. "I may be a romantic, Gleb, but one thing is definitely true. I'm the one who is here, now; the one committed to this quest. I'm the one who found you, and you'll have to deal with *me*, like it or not. The only way I can do things is my way."

Gleb's smile faded as he studied Ivan intently. "The hard way, you mean."

"The right way. Or so I hope."

Gleb shook his head. "You're just like the rest of them, chasing after a pretty face. Don't tell me that rumors of her beauty didn't attract you. Don't tell me that you, like all the other young men, don't desire to—"

Ivan lifted his chin. "She is a young girl in Kashchey's power. He's using her, whether she knows it or not. This makes her fate even worse. The virgins' souls die quickly as he devours them, but hers must perish slowly, year by year, with every sacrifice she must conduct in his name."

Gleb's gaze wavered. "She *has* no soul, boy."

Ivan held a pause. "I must try to reach her. I wouldn't

feel right if I didn't. Besides, going through her might give us some advantage over Kashchey. I heard they're very close."

Gleb crossed his arms on his chest. "We're wasting time with idle talk, boy. It's impossible to see the Mistress. She lives in a high tower in the Tzar's castle. She only comes out under heavy guard when necessary, for her Solstice duties. Or, sometimes, she turns into a dove and flies around. But then, you could never recognize her."

"A dove?" Ivan stared.

Gleb sighed. "Haven't you ever heard of shape-shifters?"

"She's a shape-shifter?"

"She can only take two forms. Human and dove. And—heed this—when she's in bird form, she has the *feelings* of a dove."

"So?"

"Have you ever heard of birds being prone to emotion?"

"The villagers call doves 'birds of love'," Ivan said uncertainly.

"Only in mockery." Gleb shook his head. "They look lovely, that's all. Don't let yourself be fooled by looks."

"She must do something else," Ivan insisted. "Doesn't she ever have... fun?"

Gleb sighed and turned to Wolf.

"I don't know why you brought him here. The boy knows nothing. You could have at least found a warrior, like the others. This one just wants to talk. And you, best of all, should know that talking won't help. It never does."

Wolf stirred, but it was Ivan who spoke.

"You speak true, old father. I'm no warrior. Yet, I'm the one you have, now. I came to you because Wolf believes I can learn from you. He believes with your help I can succeed. Will you not help?"

There was a long pause.

"Why him?" Gleb asked.

Wolf growled. In the darkness of the room his eyes shone like two hot coals. "Because he's not like the others. And the others have all failed."

"But he—"

Wolf's stare cut Gleb's words off like a knife. "I know what you are risking. If we fail, if Kashchey learns you are helping us, you won't stand a chance. Yet, the Gleb I used to know wouldn't be afraid to help the right cause. Perhaps you are not the man we sought, after all. Years have turned you into a coward."

The old man lifted his chin, the fire in his eyes more frightening than the wolf's.

"You know this is madness," he said. "Years have turned you blind, Wolf. And yet—" He turned and gave Ivan a long look. "You really believe this boy can succeed?"

Wolf sat up. "Tell him, Gleb. Tell him everything you know."

MARYA

My handwoman, Praskovia, was tall and handsome. In her late forties she still maintained the passionate vigor of a young girl, so unlike the calm detachment I had to uphold. We made a good match.

I was once told that Praskovia was the only woman who had survived my father's passions and come out of the experience intact. I heard it whispered that she could even be my mother. I didn't care. There were too many women in my father's life for me to keep track of. Their lives were too short and miserable to be worth noticing. I had more important things to do.

"The village is called *Sosnovka*, Mistress," Praskovia told me. She stood with her hands folded in front, palms together, in the ritual gesture of a Solstice priestess.

"The pine village."

"Yes, Mistress." Praskovia bowed her head. "It's no more than twenty-five *versts* by the main road. You'll recognize it by the pine grove nearby."

Twenty-five *versts* meant half a day of travel with a wagon in tow. We had to leave very early to make it back by nightfall. Still, fair was fair. Each village had to have an equal chance, no matter how far it was from the capital.

"The villagers know who they want me to take?" I asked.

It didn't matter. If they hadn't prepared an acceptable maiden to be taken, all the worse for them. I had the authority to pick any one I liked. Still, it was good to know in advance. I didn't like to come unprepared.

"Yes, Mistress." Praskovia's eyes slid over me with a tenderness I found disturbing. I looked away. I had no room for petty human feelings. My strength was in my detachment. Anything else was the surest way into the evil clutches of Love.

"Tell them to saddle Sunset for me at dawn," I told her. "And, leave me. I will sleep now."

Sunset's auburn coat glimmered in the sun, making him glow like an ember fresh from the firepit. As the first houses of the village appeared ahead of us, I pulled him to a stop and patted his steaming neck, waiting for my guards and the wagon to catch up. I felt a pang of regret at having to break the canter, but I kept my face still as I watched them approach. I couldn't possibly show my guards that I enjoyed the ride. Besides, I had to enter the village properly, as befitted my station and my solemn task.

The pair of heavy draught horses pulling the wagon acknowledged Sunset with brief snorts as they worked their way up the muddy track. This village was no different from others. Peasants in our kingdom never took time to fix the roads.

Rows of log houses lined the street, their dark windows gaping at us like ethereal eyes. No one came out to greet us, and this absence of welcome, while natural, made me feel eerie as I rode on, finding reassurance in the smacking sound of the horses' hooves and cursing of the wagon driver behind.

I had never been to this particular village, but I knew where we were headed. The well.

A small crowd gathered there watched us in silence. Mostly old crones, undoubtedly there since morning to gossip about my arrival. I rode up to them feeling mild relief that the village was not deserted as it originally seemed. I followed their unspoken signs, falling into the familiar game. No one would openly point me to the maiden, yet they all knew I must find her, and their looks, their gestures, aided me every step of the way.

A tall matron, her round face peeking out of a wrapped headscarf like a hen out of its nest, glanced at me briefly and slid her gaze toward a pair of younger women down a side street. They all looked solemn, as if attending a funeral. I signaled my wagon driver to wait and walked my horse in that direction, where the crowds thickened and the hesitant gazes of the villagers eventually led me from group to group and on to an *izba* at the end of the lane.

It was an old, crooked house. The logs composing its walls were laid unevenly, as if placed by a drunken builder. The man and woman standing in its doorway looked sad, but not desperate. They must have prepared themselves.

Good. I hated tearful scenes.

I rode up and stopped my horse in front of their rickety wooden fence.

The man gave me a long glance, his sunburnt face etched with wrinkles so deep that they made his face look like an old woodcarving. Then he turned and pulled a girl out of the darkness behind the doorway. He pushed her forward, holding her elbow from behind and I saw her stumble and wince from the force of his grip.

"Mistress, this is my youngest daughter." His voice wavered, echoed by distant sobbing from the depths of the house. The woman cast a frightened glance into the dark doorway. *Warning her other daughters not to reveal themselves to me.* I forced myself to ignore it, surveying my quarry.

She wore a plain, baggy linen dress. A dirt-gray knitted scarf covered her lowered head, hiding her hair and part of her face from view. Her eyes looked swollen and her cheeks puffed, as if she had been crying for a very long time.

"Remove your scarf," I told the girl.

She had dark blond hair, the color most common in our villages. She had pulled it all back into a tight braid, and tucked it into her dress—the usual style for a village maiden—it came in handy when they did their housework. What showed of her braid, though, looked thick enough to be pleasing when we let her hair loose on the night of the Solstice. I leaned forward in the saddle to take a closer look at her face. Her features would be pretty when she had a chance to calm down. My servants would see to it.

Under her mask of tears she looked very young and innocent, barely of age. My instincts told me she must be a virgin. The villagers must believe it too, or they wouldn't have offered her to me. After years of the Solstice Sacrifices they knew better. I saw no need to verify it on the spot, leaving the task to my women for later. No need for ugly scenes.

I straightened in my saddle, turning around to look at the frightened, expectant faces all around me. Silence wavered in the air like a heavy woolen curtain.

I felt the weight of their anxiety upon me as I turned to my guards and said: "Very well. Bring her along."

I watched my guards lead the girl into the wagon and bolt the door before mounting their heavy horses and taking positions on the outside for our long ride back. She didn't try to fight. She didn't even turn to look back as she bent her head and climbed in, settling on the straw mattress inside. Good. No trouble, then.

Sighs of relief followed me all the way to the village gate. I could still hear their echo in my head as I sent Sunset into a trot along the road, winding over the nearby hill. I shut them out as I rushed to leave the village behind.

Another gruesome task done. I did not need to dwell on it any longer.

When we finally made it back to the paved streets that led up into the palace plaza I felt exhausted. A day in the saddle, with very little food and no time for a proper rest stop took its toll. I did not look forward to facing the crowd that I knew would be waiting at the palace walls. I barely held up in my saddle, too tired to think straight. So, when a young man stepped out of the crowd right in front of my horse, it took me by surprise.

I pulled Sunset to an abrupt stop not to run this man over. My disbelief at his audacity gave way to surprise and, belatedly, to irritation as I saw my guards rushing to my side.

Dawdling fools, too slow to keep up with my horse.

Instead of cowering and retreating back into the crowd, the young villager stood his ground. My heart raced in alarm, but he showed no sign of attacking, just stood there with a smile on his face. A rather stupid smile, in fact, as if he had encountered a long-lost friend. My curiosity piqued again. A simpleton? A village idiot—likely banished from his own village for stupidity. He certainly looked the part, from his disheveled straw-colored hair, to his simple linen shirt and trousers, ragged as if he had been wearing them for months. And yet, something about his smile held my gaze. I stopped my guards, ready to trample the man, so that I could look at him just a moment longer.

His smile held childlike wonder of one beholding a miracle. It creased his freckled face and lit up his eyes, blue like cornflowers in a field of ripe wheat. I felt warmth wash over me, echoing through my tired body as I looked into those eyes. It made me feel invigorated, as if an invisible stream of power emanating from him cradled me it its beams.

I shook it off.

"You're in my way," I said.

His smile widened. "You are so beautiful."

His voice was so clear, so intense, even though he spoke quietly. It echoed through the plaza that had grown deathly still, watching us. Against reason, his words sent shivers down my spine.

I recognized trouble.

I had been complimented many times by men much more impressive than him. And yet, they'd never made me feel like this.

They'd never made me *feel*.

I struggled for words, but he seemed to have no lack of them.

"Can I come and visit you in the castle? I would very much like to get a chance to know you better."

His eyes continued to draw me in. Their cornflower blue held warmth, a mischievous vigor I had never seen before. I knew I should stop looking, but instead, I looked closer and saw something else I had missed at first. Beneath his childlike wonder, his eyes held sorrow. Old pain, surely older than he could possibly be. I felt an urge to come closer to him, to touch his hand.

Stop it, you fool. I forced my eyes away from his face and looked past him at the crowd of frozen onlookers, then at my nearest guard.

"Don't harm him," I said. "Just get him out of my way."

I urged Sunset to side-step the man and continue on towards the palace. A whip cracked behind me, followed by a grunt and gasps in the crowd, but I never looked back.

My room occupied the entire floor of the East Tower of the palace. Its gray, roughly hewn walls lay in a circle, covered by plain hangings to keep out the worst of the drafts. As I stepped in, smells of herbs, stone, and old parchment enfolded me, soothing and familiar like welcoming hands. Calm spread over me as I glanced around at the simple furnishings, the things necessary for my life and my magic. Basic, essential things, nothing that could induce feeling, that could bond me in any way. A low wooden bed; shelves of books running along the wall; a tall dark wardrobe in the corner; a massive chest between two narrow windows bearing the sacred objects for the Solstice Ceremony; the Mirror in its dark wooden frame, between the shelves and the door. And, of course, Raven's perch, a large, gnarled branch of an ancient tree fixed above the shelf in the corner.

Raven didn't stir when I walked in. He could be a very sound sleeper when he wanted. I wished my serving women had his tact and could sense my need for solitude as they fussed over me, taking off my dirt-stained cloak and preparing a bath for my tired feet. The bath was welcome, actually, but I was still relieved when they finally departed, leaving me alone with Praskovia.

"You look tired, Maryushka," Praskovia took the thick

wooden comb to my hair as I sat on a chair, relaxing my back, sore from the day in the saddle, against its smooth, polished wood. She didn't often use my childhood nickname, and just by this address I realized how worn I must look.

I wished I could forget who I was and hide my face in Praskovia's large bosom, like I sometimes had when I was a child. Or, at least, sit with her like we used to, and talk about what was on my mind. But how could I tell her that I had been shaken by a daft villager down at the plaza? What would she think of me then? She was right. I was tired. After a day's worth of travel I had every reason to be.

"It was a long ride," I told her.

"You need to eat," Praskovia said. "You are so pale. Let me send someone up with a bowl of borscht."

I considered it. She was right, again. I probably needed to eat. But I felt no hunger. And I couldn't bear to think of the fussy kitchen maids invading my room with their cheerfulness that they tried so hard to hide in my presence.

"Maybe later," I said. "I want to be alone."

She stood for a moment, looking at me. I sensed her worry, but I distanced myself from it. I had had enough of emotion for one day.

When I failed to meet her gaze, Praskovia turned and walked towards the door with smooth, graceful steps. She must have been quite a beauty in her youth. I wondered if I would look like her when I got older.

When the door closed behind her, I went straight to my Mirror. Its surface was misty-gray, reflecting nothing until a request was made. As usual, I started with the one I had been asking the Mirror ever since I was twelve.

"Show me the most beautiful woman in the world."

The gray mist thinned and disappeared, revealing my own face. I knew I would see myself, and I could have simply asked the Mirror to show my reflection, but what fun would that be? Pride was an emotion far enough from love to allow me to indulge in its simple pleasures. I smiled, and my face in the Mirror smiled back at me, pale and powerful. Mistress of the Solstice. Daughter of Kashchey.

"Show me my thoughts," I told the Mirror absentmindedly, watching the reflection of a tiny vertical line in the middle of my forehead where the dark arches of my eyebrows came together, a line that hadn't been there before. My face disappeared, the gray mist wavering beneath the smooth surface of the glass, and then...

I was staring into a pair of shiny eyes, blue like cornflowers, innocent like a child's. His freckled face was smiling, his straw hair standing on end just the way it had on the plaza. His lips moved, mutely uttering the stupid phrase from before: "You are very beautiful." And a spark in the depth of his eyes pierced me to my very soul.

"Stop!" I drew back, nearly tripping over my feet in my haste. My heart pounded as I watched his face melt away into the mist.

The Raven awoke on his perch and shrieked, but I could see nothing except the cornflower eyes, could hear nothing except his soft voice, which sent shivers through my body: "beautiful, beautiful, beautiful..."

"How dare he!" I whispered. "How dare he tell me I am beautiful!"

"Because you are beautiful, Marya," Raven replied in a hoarse whisper. "The most beautiful maiden in the world."

"I am not a maiden!" I retorted. Maidens are virgins, and by my father's Death I was not a virgin! *I will not be caught by those bonds!*

I wished I could see Father, draw strength from his pale, handsome face; let the light in his hawk-like eyes drive the memory of silly cornflowers right out of my head. I wanted to go to him, to touch his hand, to hear his calming voice. But I didn't dare. I didn't want to show him my weakness.

I knew what I had to do.

IVAN

Her eyes...

Their green was like water, deep and treacherous, with silky weeds at the bottom that could hold you to your death in their sweet embrace. They were the eyes of a sorceress, powerful and merciless; the eyes of the most beautiful woman in the world. And so much more...

He saw a vulnerability inside her eyes that held him tighter than her beauty, stronger than her commanding power. Behind her mask of cold detachment, he saw a pure, innocent soul, trapped like a bird beating in its tight impenetrable cage. It called to him, and in his heart he gave it a promise, which he was now bound to keep, just like his promise to Wolf, just like his silent oath to the fathers and brothers of the virgins sacrificed every year in the Solstice rites.

He had no choice now.

He had to save her too.

"No more talking with *her*, I hope," Wolf said.

Ivan raised his arm and looked at the crimson whip mark that creased his skin from wrist to elbow. "Gleb was right. So were you."

Wolf edged forward and paused just short of touching, his muzzle very close to Ivan's ear. "She is like that, you know. She never allows herself to care for anything or anyone. This is what makes her so powerful."

"Right." Ivan slowly got to his feet and shook off bits of the forest debris.

Wolf watched him intently. "Ready?"

"Always." Ivan's smile seemed forgotten on his face. The way he stared into the darkness of the firs made Wolf doubt the boy was seeing their prickly fingers barring his way.

Not a good frame of mind for Leshy's deadly game.

"Are you sure?" Wolf asked. "I can't guess these riddles for you, you know. And if you lose—"

"I will become a kikimora. Yes, I know."

"Kikimoras are not just swamp spirits. They remember who they used to be. They have full awareness of what they lost. And when you hear that hysterical laughter... they're not laughing for joy."

As if in response, a wail rose in the distance—a gurgling, sick laughter, interlaced with such pain and anguish that Wolf saw goose flesh rise on Ivan's arms.

"I think I get the idea," Ivan said.

"Good. You do remember what I taught you, right?"

"For the moment." Ivan raised his arms in front of his face to protect it from the drooping fir branches and dove into their dark shelter, disappearing from view.

"Good luck," Wolf called out.

There was a crackle and a muffled curse.

"Thanks!" Ivan's voice said eventually. It sounded faint, coming from a distance.

The boy knew how to move fast when he wanted to. He was good. Wolf hoped he was good enough.

The swamp looked eerie in the waning light. Ivan crept forward, painfully aware of the smacking sound his feet made on the wet grass. Among the deadly stillness of the gnarled trees draped by the curtains of the long lichen beards, his footsteps rang as loud as the church bells on a clear summer day.

Not that he had hoped to creep up on Leshy unawares.

He came to a small grass-covered clearing where the ground seemed firmer, a little island in the outskirts of the swamp. This had to be a good place.

Ivan settled on a fallen birch trunk, among its fleshy protrusions of wood ear.

"Just call him," Wolf had said. "Leshy loves to play the game. He will come."

But how did one "just call" the mighty spirit of the forest, one of the most ruthless among the Immortals?

Ivan raised his head and shouted into the still night air: "Leshy! Come out, Forest Father! I am here to play!"

"Ay! ay! ay!. . ." said the echo.

In the light of the rising moon Ivan could clearly see through the sickly swamp forest, but he could barely make out the bushes next to him. He tried to listen, but all he could hear was the buzz of a lonely mosquito in its determined attack on Ivan's neck. He waved it away. After a while the sound came back, closer, more insistent, and he turned, trying to catch the annoying insect.

Then he heard a laugh.

It was no more than a giggle, full of merriment and mischief. It almost made Ivan smile in an inadvertent desire to join in the fun. Then, as the sound sank in, he felt the skin on his back creep.

He turned slowly toward the small *beresklet* bush that had been looming over his shoulder ever since he sat down on the fallen birch trunk. The moon was high enough now to make out a pair of glistening eyes, a bulb of a nose, a mischievous grin—

A face, framed by a thick crown of leaves.

The old man straightened out from his crouch and walked from behind the dead tree onto the open grass.

"I thought you were going to let me freeze back there, boy," Leshy said. "It surely took you a long time to notice me."

His voice croaked like that of an ancient, but at the same time it was so cheerful and energetic that, against reason, Ivan smiled.

"Hello, old father," he said, doing his best to sound casual, as if talking to a forest spirit had nothing to it. "I thought you weren't coming."

"What, to miss a chance to play riddles with someone who

thinks himself clever enough for the old man?" Leshy chuckled and settled down on an old stump.

Now that Ivan could better see the Forest Man, it was hard to understand how he could have mistaken him for a bush. His clothes were similar to the kind worn in villages— a long linen shirt tied at the waist with a rope, baggy pants, and *lapti*—the wicker shoes held in place by pieces of string wrapped around the ankles. His hat was woven out of fresh twigs that looked like they were still growing, and the rope at his waist seemed to have a fringe of green leaves but, all in all, the outfit didn't seem that unusual.

Leshy's face was a different matter. It looked like a crude woodcarving, rough and grotesque. Dark, deeply set eyes glistened from underneath bushy lichen eyebrows. A bulb-like nose hung over the crack of a nearly lipless mouth. Ivan couldn't tell if the Forest Man had any hair. All he could see was a wavering mass of long *beresklet* leaves with pink-and-red splotches of berries glimmering from his neck and shoulders like delicate pieces of jewelry. They made a strange contrast with the bark-like skin.

"So, what is your name, brave boy?" Leshy asked.

"Ivan."

The old man chuckled. "I must have at least a dozen Ivans lurking out in the swamp, boy. You must have a nickname of some sort, eh? Something to tell you apart from my other kikimoras?"

Ivan sighed. It never had been easy to tell his nickname to strangers. "Ivan the Fool."

Leshy threw his head back, shaking with gurgling laughter. "The fool, eh? You do know the rules of my game?"

"Yes. I have to guess three riddles. Then I can ask you anything I want."

"Wrong!" Leshy chuckled again, laughter dancing off his skin. "*Then,* if you don't guess, I get to play with you in my swamp. I do ooh sooo need a new playmate. The other ones are becoming oooh sooo boooring...Although, a fool? I don't know."

He snapped his fingers and a pale wavering shape appeared in front of him, a ghostly outline of a naked hairy man. Once, this man must have been big and strong. Ivan could see it in the set of his square shoulders, in the way wiry muscle sculpted its way along his long arms, in the way he crouched, trying in vain to look shorter than his master. His skin hung in folds, as if he had lost a lot of weight in a very short time. His haunted wild eyes watched Leshy the way a dog might watch its abusive master raise a stick.

Ivan could see the dim outline of the forest through his misty body.

"What do you say, Nikola the Wise?" Leshy asked. "Want to play with Ivan the Fool here? Is he smart enough for us?"

For a moment, the shadow man looked at Ivan with an inexplicable plea in his eyes. Then, just as suddenly, his face twisted into a laughing grimace and he produced a long, gurgling wail.

Only a very sick man would take the sound for laughter. Nikola the Wise's ghostly face spoke of nothing but agony. The laughter made it worse.

"That's enough!" Leshy commanded. He snapped his fingers and the kikimora was gone. "I think he likes you," he added, throwing Ivan another mischievous glance.

Ivan took a much-needed breath. "Are we playing or not?"

Leshy regarded him for a moment, his eyes glistening from deep within their bushy sockets. "What could Ivan the Fool want so badly that he would risk coming here to play with the old man?" he mused. "What could be so important that the fool of a boy isn't even afraid of our old Nikola the Wise, a learned man who came to my swamp thinking he could guess any riddle in the world?"

"I'll tell you what I want," Ivan promised, "after I guess your riddles, old father."

Leshy chuckled again. "You must have a beast of a father, boy, if you think old Leshy is anything like him."

My father, Ivan thought. *My sweet, old, gullible father. You have no idea, old man.*

27

He waited.

"I have taken a liking to you, fool boy," Leshy finally said. "I will let you change your mind if you want."

Ivan shot him a glance. "Afraid to lose?"

The Forest Man was silent for a moment. "Very well," he said in a grave voice. "Listen carefully to your first riddle. I will only say it once."

MARYA

Few people know that immortality comes with a price. Every Immortal has a bane, a magical item that can render him helpless and force him to do someone else's bidding. The Immortals guard their banes closely, making sure that no one else knows what they are or where they could be found. But secrets leak out. They always do.

I know that Raven's bane is a net, one that can capture him and hold him helpless until the Net's wielder releases him. He can be captured for ages if need be. And he must do whatever the one who captured him wishes. Such are the rules of his immortality.

I have no idea where Raven keeps his bane and who guards it against the chance fortune-seekers. His secret is safe, for his powers are not as desired as those of Yaga, or Domovoi, or Zmei Gorynych, the Fire Serpent. Raven cannot grant you riches, glory, or long life. His true price is in the knowledge he possesses. But very few know even that much about him.

When my father created the Needle with his death at its tip, he wanted to present it as a bane, so that he can be talked of as a true Immortal like the others. But his secret leaked out, just like all of them do. His Needle is no bane, for it cannot render him helpless or force him to do anyone's bidding. Nor is my father a true Immortal, for breaking the Needle would kill him. He had tried to keep this secret too, and failed.

29

IVAN

He recalled bits of his earlier conversation with Gleb.

"Rendering Raven helpless is only part of the task," Gleb had said. "You must force him to reveal the information to you, and that could be harder than Leshy's games."

"Wouldn't he be bound to do what I ask?" Ivan had frowned as Wolf snorted on his mat by the fire, hiding his muzzle in his folded paws. "Did I say something funny?"

Ivan had been so tired of this conversation, where Gleb and Wolf seemed to bounce inaudible jokes back and forth, making Ivan feel more and more clueless as the old herb man revealed more and more information to him.

"Couldn't Wolf question Raven once we catch him?" he had asked.

"This is your quest, boy," Wolf had said, even as Gleb shook his head. "Rules are rules, sorry."

Back then, Ivan had left it at that, knowing that he wouldn't learn anything more this time. In any case, capturing Raven seemed like a distant, unattainable goal. No one he knew of had ever bested Leshy at his riddle game. Most likely Ivan would be a kikimora by morning and none of this would be necessary. And if he did succeed, if he managed to render Raven helpless and bound to do Ivan's bidding, surely he could get what he wanted out of the old bird.

He would have all the time in the world to do it.

MARYA

"It is your time to hunt," I told Raven.

He nodded, his dry, glistening eye piercing me from its feathered frame. Then he spread his wings and floated out of the window.

I knew he would fly through the night forest without touching a single branch on his way. He would hunt, and eat his fill. And then, he would go to the lake and float over its mirror waters to the edge of the swamp and back, until the first light of dawn touched the sky in the east. As I watched his black winged shape melt into the moonlit air outside the window, I briefly wondered what bonded him to these waters, forcing him into this nightly ritual. But I knew he'd never tell me.

When I was little, I used to question and plead with him until my voice grew hoarse. Now, I didn't bother anymore.

Especially not tonight, when I had a more important task on my hands.

I turned to the Mirror and straightened out my dress. "Show me my reflection."

I cannot be bonded by love. All my life is devoted to staying detached from its destructive power. When I find myself dangerously concerned with thoughts of a man, I know a perfect remedy.

I go and share my bed with another.

I know my enemy enough to understand this. Love is sensual, but its sensuality has nothing to do with feelings, with a true bonding of two souls meant to be together for eternity. While many mistake sensuality for love, I, Mistress of the Solstice, know better. To keep myself free from falling in love, I have long learned to divide the desires of my body and mind, to separate them so that they would be weaker and easier to defeat. If my mind is set on one man, my body must find a different one to satisfy its urges.

The act throws you off for a while, giving you an odd sense of duality. It makes you float between earth and sky, blown back and forth by emotions, like winds on all sides. You lose the subject of your love in a blur that is all men in the world, a blur of arms, bodies, caresses. Love is pain, and this simple recipe allows you to numb it until you sort things out.

In the end, it works like a charm.

I needed somebody different. Somebody I had never met before, an outsider who wouldn't be intimidated by my station. Somebody strong and experienced, who would make me forget my unnatural fancy. This close to the Solstice I couldn't afford to take any risks.

To seek a man outside the palace I had to look like a commoner, a village girl adventurous enough to run away from her parents to attend her first Solstice. There were always such maidens, girls who act under the perception that the coming Solstice breaks all boundaries. These girls are common objects of protection for wandering knights, and easy prey for passionate men.

Like an artist I painted my new appearance, sparing no detail. My black hair became reddish brown, shorter—about waist-long—and curlier. Pretty, but not too beautiful, young, but mature enough for a chance affair. My eyes remained green, though I gave them a touch of brown at the edges. I shaped my eyelashes shorter and lighter, aiming for the subtle look of adventurous inexperience.

A brown dress over a green undergarment, its neckline low enough to show a little cleavage, completed the outfit. Looking over my final appearance, I added some fullness and color to my cheeks and decided that it would do.

Wrapped in a dark cloak, I made my way outside the castle. Guards dozed near the entrance to the front courtyard. I sent them a calming thought and made them look the other way as I slid past them, treading noiselessly on the cold stone pavement.

The tavern I chose was far enough from the palace not to run into any familiar guards, but close enough for an easy walk and, as I knew from my previous forays, popular with adventurers and fortune-seekers. Its huge common room was full, bathed in lantern lights that focused on its center, leaving the corners in the shadow. Thick vapors of ale, sweat, and cheap stew hung in the air like a curtain. Bits of conversations floated up through the background hum that from time to time exploded here and there with roars of quarrel or thunders of laughter.

Smells and sounds rushed forth to enfold a newcomer into their breathtaking cocoon. I paused in the doorway, adjusting my assaulted senses to a new level of tolerance.

It was the time of night when ale gets into heads, and the boundaries between acceptable and outrageous stretch to a breakage point. The few women scattered throughout the room had already lost all reserve, draping over their chance companions like bundles of wet cloth. A group of rogues in the proximity of the counter shouted profanities at an ugly serving wench, laughing so vigorously that the ale in their mugs spilled across the floor.

Along with everyone else in the room, they turned to look at the new addition to their late-night merriment. Their gazes slid over me like thick, oiled fingers, reaching as far inside as my outfit would allow. The force of the sensation made me shudder.

I ran my gaze over the worst our kingdom's manhood had to offer. One good lover was all I needed. There had to be one among them that I could use. I forced my eyes to move slowly, not to turn away from anyone, even as the filth of their gazes brought inadvertent color to my cheeks.

A group in the corner looked somewhat better than the

others. Their clothes, one step above peasant dress, showed a reasonable effort toward cleanliness. The one on the right looked less drunk than the others, and as my gaze caught his I saw a gleam of interest that went beyond plain lust. He was less than I'd hoped for, though. Certainly not the seducer I needed today.

I ran another hopeless glance around the room. And then I saw him. Late twenties, dark, lean, muscular. Handsome, but not overly so. He leaned out of the shadow in the corner, watching me with interest. I met his eyes, then blushed and looked away.

His eyes bore into me with burning intensity. My heart raced with anticipation. Forcing the images of cornflowers and straw, of smiles and sunshine out of my head, I studied the positions of the future participants in my little play. I measured distances, estimated the approximate times my actors needed to enter the stage. Excitement rose in my chest, the tingling feeling a fighter must enjoy when his sword leaves the sheath to rejoin his hand. It had been a while since I had gone on a man-hunt. I didn't realize how much I missed it.

The rogues at the counter were very drunk by now. The man I was aiming for was sitting a little too far away for my liking, but it had to do. I chose a lonely spot in between the counter and my future hero, and fluttered my hand in a shy, hopeless gesture the servers were bound to miss. Sure enough, the wench, annoyed by the rudeness of the rogues near the bar, kept clear of our corner, turning her back with a determined set of her bony shoulders.

I waved some more, after making sure the wench was otherwise occupied. I tried not to look at the rogues as I counted under my breath, cursing the ale for clouding their head. Was my plan going to work? Or were they all too drunk already?

The nearest rogue swayed and finally turned my way. His red face was so swollen with ale that his beady eyes almost drowned in their sockets. He had a glassy look, as if not fully aware of his surroundings. Yet, as he focused on my face— or, rather, my cleavage—his expression acquired some sense.

He even winked to me, a pitiful attempt at flirting as he took another swig from his mug.

"Barman!" he yelled at the top of his lungs.

Everyone in the proximity turned their heads to us. My future hero in his corner raised his head and I prayed he wasn't going to rush to my rescue before time. I settled deeper into my chair, pulling my shawl tighter around my shoulders.

"This beauty here needs a drink!" The rogue's thunderous voice shook the air, too loud for my heightened senses. "Come here, wench!"

I blushed, putting on a look of uneasiness. He struggled to his feet and swayed, to the laughter and cheers from his comrades. My heart raced. *It's not going to work. He's too drunk.*

I waved my hands in pretended agitation, making awkward attempts to push away without getting up from my seat and in the struggle letting my shawl slide off my shoulders to the floor. As I bent to pick it up, I revealed a glimpse of my breasts to the rogue, at the same time looking up at him with the helplessness that this type of man finds inviting. That gave him the necessary boost. He fought his way out of his seat and rushed toward me, bumping into tables and chairs, his drunken companions laughing at his back.

His condition worked in my favor. Barely able to walk straight, he posed no real threat, but he would look sufficiently dangerous to a frightened village girl. I backed away to the nearest wall, pressing against it, leaving myself open for him to do his worst.

I pretended to struggle as he tore at my dress, leaving a gaping hole. He reached for my hair, grabbing the comb that held it in place and freeing my hair to flow loose, the reddish-brown curls tumbling down to my waist. I didn't resist as he savaged my carefully prepared outfit. The only thing I didn't let him do was leave any marks on me. I had to look my best for later.

I hadn't realized that the man I'd picked for myself was such a good fighter. He jumped from his corner, swift as lightning, and struck down my attacker with a single blow. Three rogues came to the aid of the fallen man, and he knocked each of them down with quick punches, aimed so expertly that none of his opponents even let out a sound. Not bothering to see if any of them would rise, he turned to me as I was standing against the wall trembling, tears running down my face.

"You are so brave... sir," I whispered, holding my scarf over my torn blouse.

"You shouldn't be alone in such a place," he said with concern. "Let me walk you home... or wherever it is you're staying."

"Thank you, sir." I reached out for his offered hand and drew back again, as one of the tears in my dress gaped.

He kept his eyes discreetly lowered. "You're in no shape to go outside."

"I have my needlework with me," I whispered. "If I could only find a place to repair my dress, I could do it in no time."

"I'm staying in this tavern," he replied gently. "Would you consider going to my room? I promise you will be safe there."

I looked into his eyes and smiled. A smile of trust. Of hidden promise.

"You are my savior," I said. "I trust you with my life and honor."

IVAN

Leshy's voice echoed clearly through the night forest as he recited his first riddle:

"A delicate basket, I shimmer with light.
Yet I am so strong, it is useless to fight.
The longer you struggle, the tighter my hold,
And when I release you, I also unfold."

Ivan paused, recalling everything he had learned about the game. "There're rules to these riddles," Wolf had told him. "First, the answer is a common, everyday thing that everyone knows. Second, each riddle has only one answer that fits everything in the rhyme. And, third, to compensate for the ease of the first two, some of them are very confusingly phrased. Think before you answer, boy." The warning didn't seem necessary. Ivan was willing to think as hard as he could to avoid Nikola the Wise's fate. Yet, no matter how hard he thought of it, there seemed to be only one answer.

"Spider web," he said.

Leshy's look held mischief, but deep inside, Ivan also saw disappointment.

"The Fool, the boy calls himself," Leshy mused. "A tricky fool." His eyes shimmered in the eerie swamp light. "I always use the easy one first," he added.

Ivan knew this didn't have to be true. Yet, he also knew each new riddle would be harder than the previous one. Leshy liked to play. And he didn't like to lose.

"Listen, fool boy," Leshy said.

"I flow like a river, I wash like a sea,
I circle and circle, and never I flee.
The aim of your life is to keep me contained,

For death will you meet if I roam undetained."

Ivan thought hard. Common, everyday things, Wolf had said. What sort of a common, everyday thing could flow like a river, yet mean death if it roamed undetained? Water?

But it was hardly the aim of anyone's life to keep it contained. No more was it true that water never fled. Perhaps Leshy was referring to an ocean?

Many storytellers spoke about the sea, a great pond of water without shores that led to wondrous kingdoms and magical lands. Some of these tales mentioned "ocean", the grand pond of water that collected the seas into itself to wash their waters around the edge of the world. Surely water this wide would cause anyone's death if ever allowed to roam free.

But a common, everyday thing? Hardly.

I flow like a river, I wash like a sea,
I circle—
What could it possibly be?

Ivan sighed. *Don't give in to the panic. Fear is your enemy. Fear is what Leshy hopes for. Fear is the making of a kikimora—*
Stop.
Concentrate.
Flow. Wash. Circle. Yet, not water. What else can possibly do all these things?

Ivan glanced at Leshy. The Forest Man was busy, poking at one of the wood ears that creased the fallen birch trunk with a knobby finger. Each time he poked, a dimple appeared on the surface under his finger. Ivan imagined he could see movement.

He looked closer and drew back in disgust.

The wood ear was an opalescent mass of worms that glistened faintly in the light of a rising moon. Breaking off from the lump, the worms dug under the white birch bark to reemerge inches away, like divers that swim underwater and pop out their heads to see where they are.

Ivan moved away along the log. A whole section of it collapsed to become a crawling mass of worms that spread out and poured over the edge of the swamp-island to disappear into the dark glistening water.

Leshy giggled.

"How's the riddle comin', smart boy? Ready or not, it's time!"

Ivan took a breath.

Don't show your fear. Leshy feeds on fear. Don't—

But what should I do?

"Come, boy!" Leshy said. "There's no shame in losing. Think of all the fun we could have out here in my swamp! Just you and me, eh? You have but to say the word to the old man."

He beamed and crept along the log closer to Ivan. For the first time Ivan noticed the chill the Forest Man emanated. Or, perhaps, the chill hadn't been there before?

A sting in his hand made him look down. A mosquito, perhaps the very same one that had bothered him earlier, was using Ivan's stillness to feed on his hand. Ivan smashed the annoying insect, leaving a splash of blood on his pale skin.

He raised his hand to rub the blood off, and paused.

The aim of your life is to keep me contained.

Of course. What kind of a fool was he, to think so long?

"Blood," he said.

Leshy cocked his head to one side.

"Fancy," he said. "How careless people are when dealing out nicknames. If I remember correctly, our good Nikola the Wise met his doom upon the very same riddle. He kept blabbering about an ocean or something. Why, I don't even know what an 'ocean' is...Blood. Hmmm."

Leshy glanced at a small fir tree rising out of the swamp. There was a barely audible sound, like a breath drawn in, and the tree withered right in front of Ivan's eyes. The fresh green needles turned yellow, then brown, and then crumpled off the branches, suddenly thinned and gnarled like an old woman's hands. Leshy watched with a cold gleam of satisfaction in his eyes. Then he turned to Ivan and gave him a meaningful look.

"All right, Ivan the Fool of a Misleading Nickname," he said, "since you're so good at riddles, I'll give you my hardest one yet. No one has ever been able to guess this one. Off the top of my head, I don't even think I recall the answer myself." He giggled.

Ivan took care not to show any reaction. Intimidating an opponent was an ancient and effective tactic. He had been told that Leshy used it a great deal. The best way to handle it was not to pay any attention. If he could manage to do so.

He listened.

"I'm always a welcome one, always a treasure,
Yet sometimes resented beyond any measure.
But when I decide that I must slip away,
You'll fight to return me, you'll beg me to stay."

Ivan took a breath. "Only one answer," Wolf had said. Which meant, among other things, that there had to *be* an answer.

"Always welcome" yet "sometimes resented". What could it be?

A child?

Most people he knew welcomed children, yet some would do anything to avoid having one; such as, a family with too many mouths to feed; or a maiden who had ruined her prospects of a good marriage by being a bit too careless in her adolescent games.

There went the "always welcome" part, and with it went the answer itself. However confusing, everything in the riddle had to be consistent with the sole answer that fit all parts of the rhyme.

If, of course, Leshy always followed the rules. According to Wolf, it was a given. Yet, watching the shifting moods on Leshy's face, it was easy to suspect foul play.

"I'm beginning to freeze, boy," Leshy complained. He cast his eyes on a nearby puddle of swamp water. After a brief moment, steam started to rise off its still surface. By the time Ivan caught his breath, the water was boiling like soup in a kettle. The pale shape of a dead frog floated up and disappeared back in the turmoil.

Concentrate.

"He will do anything to distract you," Wolf had said. "Don't let him. That's how he wins."

Leshy looked away, and the water slowly calmed again. The faint smell of fish soup tainted the air, topped by the heady aroma of wild rosemary on a hot day.

"I don't understand it, boy. Why do you resist your fate so much? It's so nice and cozy here in the swamp. We're all so looking forward to playing with a sweet one like you... You do like to play, don't you, boy?" He crept a few inches toward Ivan.

The chill he'd emanated earlier was gone. Instead, Ivan caught the scent of *beresklet* berries—flowery and bitter at the same time. The faint smell of stale water gave the *beresklet* scent a moldy touch, but Ivan couldn't tell if it was coming from Leshy himself, or from the swamp around them.

He did his best to ignore the old man and focus on the riddle.

What was it that everyone welcomed and treasured and yet sometimes resented beyond measure? What was it that one would do anything to keep when it decided to slip away?

Love?

Yes, it seemed likely.

"Ready yet?" Leshy asked.

Yes, Ivan almost said, but something held him.

Think some more. You only get this one shot.

"Oh, come now," The Forest Man pouted. "Why d'you insist on being sooo boring?... It is so beautiful here at night. Once you sees it, you'll never want to leave!"

He swept his hands, as if opening an invisible curtain. Suddenly the air filled with swarms of fireflies. They looked like fairies; at a distance Ivan could imagine seeing them carry small lanterns in their delicate hands. It became bright like daylight. Ivan could even see faint rainbows shining in the glassy wings.

"See?" Leshy said by his ear. He was so close that Ivan jumped, his heart pounding. *How did he get behind me?* He suppressed the urge to draw away, to show his fear.

The Forest Man reached a finger past Ivan and poked the nearest flying shape. With a faint pop it burst apart, splashing Ivan with a tiny droplet of goo.

It took all the courage Ivan had to keep still as the beautiful fairy-like creatures popped all around him, leaving behind ugly reddish splotches that looked so much like blood.

The light faded.

"Aaah," Leshy sighed. "I could do this all night long. Such fun, these light beasties, don't you find?" He turned to Ivan and gave him one of his mischievous grins. "Ready yet?"

Ivan swallowed. He had almost forgotten about the riddle. Wolf had warned him, and yet, it had been so hard—

Think. Concentrate.

Was "love" the answer to the last riddle?

Love was certainly a feeling everyone welcomed and treasured, and certainly one that from time to time brought more pain than happiness. Yet, from all Ivan knew about love, there was never a time for it to slip away. True love was the most permanent thing he knew. Except, perhaps, time itself.

Of course, there were many ways to look at love, including the sickly sacrifice done in the name of love that dominated this kingdom. But Ivan firmly believed one thing: true love, if one ever had the privilege to experience it, was stronger than anything in the world.

Even stronger than death.

And then he knew.

He turned to Leshy and met the old man's eyes.

"Life," he said.

There was a pause. A long one.

"I lied," Leshy told him. "This wasn't my hardest riddle. In fact, it was an easy one. Care to try again?"

Ivan smiled, relief washing over him. He didn't realize how tense he had been until he felt his hands tremble from the released stress.

"I suppose not," Leshy mumbled. "Of course, I didn't really want you in my swamp, boy. What would I do with such a smart one as you? What would my sweet Nikola think of one who'd cracked the very same riddle that brought about his doom, without as much as a flinch?" He paused, studying Ivan with a strange glint in his eyes. "On the bright side," he continued, "this way I gets to know what it was that prompted you to come here in the first place. Tell me, boy: what do you seek from Leshy?"

Ivan took a breath. "There is a net. A net that can capture a certain bird."

Leshy's expression was unreadable. "A bird. That's what our fool seeks. A bird. And what bird might that be, boy? A dove, perchance?" He broke out in giggles, bouncing up and down on the old log.

Ivan waited for the laughter to stop.

"A raven," he said. "There's only one such net in existence, and you have it."

"Now, now," Leshy wiped his tears, amber like drops of tree sap. "No need to get impatient. Who told you I have the Net, clever boy?"

"Someone who knows."

"Secrets, eh? 'Old father' you called me. Begged me to play. I thought we were friends now. Do friends have secrets from each other?" He looked at Ivan for a long moment.

Ivan looked back, his face carefully blank.

"All right," Leshy nodded. "Fine. Be this way." He sighed. "As it happens, I do know where the Net is. It isn't far at all. But you have to go and get it yourself, smart boy."

"Where?" Ivan suspected his trial wasn't over yet.

Leshy stretched out a hand that looked like a gnarled *beresklet* branch, warts and all. "You see that blinky light out there?"

Ivan looked. There was indeed a tiny greenish light shimmering among the swamp vapors. Cold, death-like, it was quite different from the warm firefly glow.

"It's a glowing piece of wood," Leshy said. "A rotten tree stump. One of my kikimoras—Oksana is her name—she likes to carry a light when out in the swamp. She's guarding a tree with a hole in it. Talk to her. Perchance, you could even learn her nickname. I don't recall it myself. Then, when you're done, reach into the hole if you dare, and you'll find the Net. Or find yourself without a hand." He giggled again.

Ivan ignored the last remark. No physical harm was supposed to come to him as a result of winning Leshy's game. The only thing he had to worry about was keeping his sanity.

If, of course, Leshy always followed the rules.

He had so far, hadn't he?

"Oh, yes. One more thing. You probably need a guide." Leshy snapped his fingers and the tormented shape of Nikola the Wise appeared again. The kikimora's wild eyes burned through Ivan.

"Nikola will show you a safe path through the swamp. I'm sure he'd love to. Won't you, dearie?"

Nikola's gurgling laugh choked in his throat under Leshy's heavy gaze.

"Off you go!" Leshy commanded. "Shoo!"

He stepped behind the birch log into the shadow of the fir growth. After a moment, it seemed as if there had never been anything else there but bushes, sickly from the swamp water that surrounded their exposed roots. None of them resembled *beresklet* at all.

The only reminder of the Forest Man's presence was the withered brown shape of the little fir tree and the reddish splotch of a squashed firefly on Ivan's hand. He hastily rubbed it off, and followed Nikola's ghostly shape.

At first it was easy to find a dry path. As they moved deeper into the swamp, Nikola jumped from one patch of dry land rising out of the swamp to another, and Ivan took care to copy his movements. Dark water glistened all around, like eyes peering at them through the stiff swamp grass. Nikola had no need to jump, except for Leshy's orders to show him the way. For once, Ivan appreciated the code of the Immortals and the Forest Man's care.

The island appeared from the moonlit mist like a ghostly ship, the tall aspen in its center rising like a mast out of the swamp moss. As Nikola's feet touched the island, he disappeared into thin air with a last look at his lucky follower. Ivan did his best to ignore the longing in Nikola's tortured gaze. He could do nothing about the other man's fate.

The blue-green swamp light floated toward him, so different from the yellow and red shades of a real fire. It seemed very pale, barely visible against the moonlight. Ivan realized now that it didn't really flicker. It only appeared flickering when its bearer moved.

The kikimora approached him, her ghostly shape taking on more substance with each step.

"Hello," she said. "I am Oksana. Did you come to play with me?"

A chill seized Ivan's chest and held him in a tight grip. Among all the horrors of the swamp, he had never expected to see *this*. *Gods. Gods, no. Dear, dear gods, no. Not this.*

Please, not a child.

She looked no more than five. Her eyes were so large in her pale face that they took on a life of their own, shifting and glancing around as if afraid of an ambush. There was nothing childish in their depths. They held pain. So much pain—

"Come," she beckoned. "I like company. I'm not scary, really."

Ivan swallowed.

"I came for the Net," he heard himself saying. "Leshy sent me."

She pursed her lips. "I thought you would at least like to know my nickname. Everyone else does."

Her mouth stretched into a smile, but her eyes held the same torment, the same madness he saw in Nikola's. It was a thousand times worse, seeing it in the eyes of a child.

What kind of monster could have made a kikimora out of an innocent little girl?

"All right," he said, only vaguely aware of the hoarseness of his voice. "What is your nickname?"

"Aha!" She jumped a few steps back. Her face twisted into a grimace that might have passed for laughter if not for the expression of her eyes. "I—I don't have one! I don't have a nickname!" She threw her head back and wailed, with the sound that Ivan had in the past few hours learned to call laughter. Kikimora's laughter.

He waited for her to finish and did his best not to look away.

"Then," he said quietly, "why don't we give you one?"

She looked at him with wonder. For a moment her eyes became dreamy, almost sane.

"You? You will give me a nickname?"

"Of course," he said. "Why not?"

She hesitated. "All right. But—why don't you get your Net first? Uncle Leshy won't be pleased if I keep you."

"In that case," Ivan suggested, "while I am getting the Net, why don't you think what kind of a nickname you'd like to have?"

Her eyes showed doubt. And wonder, which sparkled through the madness like a star in a stormy sky. "All right. Just don't reach all the way inside. The Net is right near the opening. And deeper inside there's the—the handcatcher!" She laughed again. This time it lasted shorter than before.

"The nickname," Ivan reminded her. "Think of the nickname."

He stepped forward and reached into the gaping hole of the tree. Oksana was right. The Net was very close to the entrance. It was soft, like a breath of warm air. So alien to the moldy swamp chill. Was this why Raven chose Leshy as a guardian of his magical bane?

Was it Raven's choice? Was he free to choose the keeper of the only item in the world that could truly harm him? Or was it forced on him by some higher powers, to maintain control over the world's order?

Did such powers truly exist?

Ivan forced the thought away as he pulled the Net out and clenched it in his fist. It was woven so finely that it could be folded to the size of a hazelnut. Partially folded, it filled his hand like a puff of warm air.

Oksana sat on the ground a few paces away, her face blank.

"Have you thought of a nickname?" he asked.

"I don't have a nickname," she said absently, as if their conversation minutes ago hadn't happened.

Ivan lowered to the ground in front of her.

"What did your mother call you?"

She looked at him, startled. Then she threw her head back, shaking with a deafening fit of laughter.

Ivan waited. He didn't look away.

MARYA

I followed my savior into warm darkness. After a patient moment I heard a match struck and soft reddish light poured into a lantern on the table.

It was a cozy room, with a small curtained window, a washbasin in the corner, and a large bed. It even had sheets made of plain, sun-bleached linen, and the pad underneath had wisps of wool mixed in with the usual mattress straw. My new acquaintance obviously liked to travel in style.

I threw a helpless glance around, pulling the scarf tighter around my savaged dress.

"You don't need to be afraid," he said gently. "Would you like me to leave?"

"No," I whispered. "I'd rather you stayed with me...sir."

I gave him a long look and noted a spark of new interest in the depth of his dark eyes. It echoed in my chest with growing excitement. The hold was established. All I had to do now was turn the spark into flame.

And hope he was as good as his looks suggested.

"My name is Kirill," he offered.

I looked at him as if deciding whether or not I could trust him. "I'm Dasha."

"Well, Dasha, why don't you sit on the bed? I'll take this chair over here."

I stepped over to the bed and stopped helplessly, as if realizing for the first time what my next difficulty was going to be. I looked down over my torn dress. Then, I raised my head and met his eyes with a hunted look.

After a moment, he saw it too.

"I can offer you my spare shirt to wear," he said with hes-

48

itation. "And, perhaps it would be better if I left you alone after all."

"No! Kirill..." I said pleadingly. "These men—they saw where I went. If you leave me alone here, they'll find me!"

"These drunkards scared you, poor child." He shook his head. "Very well. I'll stay here with you. I'll just...look away."

I held his gaze a bit longer this time, showing him a glimpse of a woman through the mask of innocence. I pitched my voice lower. "Thank you, Kirill. I feel so safe with you."

Seduction is the only love-game I am allowed, and I enjoy it very much. Nothing is more exciting than making a man want me more than anything, and then allowing him to court me and win my favor. I especially enjoy the way experienced men do it. They savor the contest itself, sparing no detail. And then, when you finally give in, they take you over completely, inside and out. Your body becomes a pure essence of ecstasy under their skillful hands. They worship you like a goddess who granted her mortal admirer a moment of her presence.

And then, when all is over, they leave you forever. For they are wanderers, seekers, and a woman is interesting to them only if she is new.

But I never wait this long. I like to leave first, before the break of dawn, before the memory grows cold on my body. I turn into a dove and fly home to my tower in the Tzar's palace. I fly above love. I fly free.

"It is done," I told Kirill.

He turned his head to see me sitting on his bed, wearing only his shirt, with the mended dress heaped in my lap in a way that left most of my legs exposed to the warm air of the room.

"Oh," he said, turning away. "Sorry. I thought you were ready."

"Almost," I told him. "I just need to put it on. But how can

I thank you for all your help?"

"No need," he assured me. "I couldn't let such a beautiful girl as you be treated so badly."

"Do you—" I held a pause, letting my breath catch in a small gasp. "Do you really think I am beautiful?"

He turned back and looked at me again as I sat there, showing no attempt to hide myself. I looked straight at him as he took in all the lines and curves only half-hidden by his loose shirt, the way the skin of my bare legs gave off a soft gleam in the reddish light of the lantern.

"Yes," he said, his voice slightly hoarse. "You are very beautiful, Dasha."

I blushed, letting the color fill my cheeks and touch seductively on my neck and chest. Yet, I kept his gaze.

"Nobody ever told me this before," I said quietly. "Not like this."

I kept still, beckoning with my eyes. He shivered as his body urged him on where his mind held him back. I set the mended dress aside and let it slide off the bed to the floor, leaving nothing between me and his hungry gaze but the thin linen of his shirt. He licked his lips as he followed the line of my neck down to where it disappeared into the shirt's wide opening. Then he tore his gaze away and looked me in the face.

"We shouldn't," he said hoarsely. "I can't take advantage of you like this."

I almost laughed at such foolish honor, but I kept my face straight. "Isn't it for me to decide?"

"But you—I—"

"Don't you like me?"

He swept over to sit next to me on the bed. "I like you very much, Dasha. I think you are exquisite. I just think you are too innocent."

Innocent. I almost laughed again, but again I kept a straight face as I reached out and touched his hand. A shudder went through his body and echoed in mine.

"I am not a virgin," I whispered, letting my eyelids drop

and a new shade of pink rush into my cheeks at this confession.

I waited. Somehow this simple piece of information often did wonders for loosing a man from his principles. I had counted to five under my breath when I felt his hand on me.

His fingers lightly traced the outside of my leg from thigh to ankle. This time my gasp wasn't pretense. I turned to him, my eyes dreamy.

His hand returned, this time pressing harder against my skin. All the while he kept my gaze, watching for signs that would caution him to stop.

I bent my head to the side, letting my loose hair slide over my shoulder, its weight caressing my arm and side. I wanted to immerse myself in his touch. But he wasn't certain yet that he could proceed.

"It feels like... bliss," I whispered, closing my eyes briefly and then opening them again to encourage him on.

He edged closer and ran his hands lightly along my arms, from fingertips to shoulders, reaching inside the wide sleeves of my borrowed shirt. Holding me inside the cloth he drew me closer. My head tipped back to expose the tender skin of my throat to his lips. His hot tongue ran along my neck down to the delightful spot where the collarbones came together.

My gasp turned into a moan. I wanted to respond, but he held me in such a way that I couldn't move my arms, couldn't do anything but submit to his caress. I gave in to it, savoring every moment.

His lips brushed the opening of my shirt, the hollow of my throat, the tops of my breasts. He shifted my weight in his arms to bring my face level with his, and drew me toward him, his breath hot on my burning skin. His mouth covered mine, his tongue parting my lips. My moan caught in my throat as he slid it inside, filling my mouth. He tasted of musk, hops, and expensive ale, its fumes rising into my head. My mouth fell open in response, my face drawing to his faster than my conscious thought.

His hands found their way under the shirt, his fingers

pressing on the right spots to evoke a response. I shivered as his touch became stronger, a powerful caress that would have seemed rough if it didn't answer so well the fire that burned inside me. I submerged into it, clinging to him, yielding my body to his fierce hands.

After a while he drew away and looked at me, as if seeing me for the first time.

"Gods," he whispered. "Dasha. I don't know what came over me. I—"

I shifted in his arms, drawing my head away just enough to focus on his face.

"Take off your clothes," I whispered. "I want you, now." My voice trembled with urgency, and he responded to it without hesitation.

I watched his muscles shift under his smooth, hairless skin as I pulled off my shirt, letting it slide off the bed down to the floor. He was more handsome than I imagined. His body was sculpted of muscle, lean and strong like a warrior's. My eyes moved lower and I blushed, bringing them back up to his face. He knew I wasn't a virgin, but now was not the time to show my experience.

"You are so beautiful, Dasha," he whispered. "You are the most beautiful woman I've ever seen."

He scooped me up in his arms and lay me down on the bed. Then he eased alongside me, running his fingers over my body in a gentle caress.

I closed my eyes and let myself float. It was bliss. It was everything I wanted. It was the best thing I'd ever felt, and I immersed myself fully in the sensation.

He knew a woman's body. His touch drove me to ecstasy, and stopped, and then drove me there again. He knew where to be gentle and where to be strong, how far to go before he stopped and went on again. I was vaguely aware of my screams. Everything else faded, leaving only the sense of touch, the most important, the only important sense in the whole world.

His insistent fingers slid inside me and I welcomed them

with a gasp that almost left me breathless. I wanted him never to stop. I yearned for him like a babe yearns for her mother's breast. And yet, I wanted more.

I stretched out my hand and touched him. As my burning fingers closed over his hardened manhood, I felt him shudder and heard him gasp. I used my free hand to draw him on top of me and guided him to where I wanted him most.

The first moment of his entry was so intense I almost lost myself in it. And then our movements, our senses, our thoughts joined into an unbearable ecstasy and beyond, into darkness.

IVΛN

Wolf raised his head at a rustling in the brush. It was about time. The moon was high, its silver light pouring down into the glade. It was nearly as bright as daylight.

When no other sound followed, Wolf almost decided to return to his slumber. Then he saw Ivan.

The boy sat by the old fir at the far end of the glade, barely visible in the deep shade of the drooping branches. He was still, staring unseeingly into the distance.

Wolf got to his feet and padded over to Ivan.

"Well?"

There was no answer. Wolf sighed, swallowing the rising worry.

"I'm pretty sure you aren't kikimora, lad. Care to tell this old beast what happened?"

Ivan rolled his eyes and opened his clenched fist.

Wolf nodded. "You got it!"

The silvery net shimmered in the moonlight. Spread out in the boy's hand it looked airy, almost insubstantial, gossamer, like a harmlessly unfolded spider web.

"Why are you just sitting here, boy?" Wolf demanded. "Get up! We have things to do!"

Ivan didn't respond.

"What did Leshy do to you?" Wolf asked, feeling the cold hand of worry grasp his heart again.

"He showed me where the Net was," Ivan said. "But I had to get it myself."

"And?"

"It was in a hole of a tree, on an island in the middle of the swamp." Ivan's voice was slow, distant. "A kikimora guarded it."

"Didn't I teach you the kikimoras cannot harm you if you come to the swamp by Leshy's bidding?"

A pause. "She was... a little girl." Ivan's adam's apple bobbed as he swallowed. "She'd gone to the swamp to play riddles, to make a wish to save her dying mother. She was five at the time. She still *looks* five." He fell silent.

Wolf fixed the boy with a long stare, his head level with Ivan's face.

"So, old Leshy spared your feelings. He didn't show you all the others—hundreds and thousands of tormented souls who bargained with him over matters of life and death, and ended up his powerless toys. He didn't show you what it takes to put the madness in their eyes, to make their memories spark that sickening laughter. He didn't tell you how he makes a kikimora, a task so cruel that even Immortals never speak of it. No, he knew how easy it was to break the spirit of a sensitive lad like you. One little girl child—and you go all mushy and decide to give up." He turned his back to Ivan and curled up on the fir-covered ground. "Why did I even bother with you?"

For a while there was no sound.

"I'm not giving up," Ivan said.

Wolf waited.

"It's just so... wrong."

Wolf turned, so that he could see the boy out of the corner of one eye. "Nobody said this was going to be easy."

"I know."

Wolf peered into the boy's face. There was more sense in Ivan's eyes. Some of his old self shone in their blue depths.

"We don't have much time, lad. We have to make it to the glade by the castle before the moon sets, remember?"

"But—" Ivan jumped to his feet, with the look of someone who has just become aware of the time. "It *is* late. How are we—"

"Hop on to my back," Wolf said.

He was glad to see the horror in Ivan's eyes. It looked like he'd managed to teach the boy proper respect after all.

"But you never—"

"Get on, boy. If all's well you can still get there before dawn."

MARYA

Kirill was insatiable. As he took me again and again with carnal passion, he drove me to the point where I could not stop either, shaking in climax after climax to his rhythmic moves. I never had such a good lover before. Or perhaps I forgot?

When he finally rolled off me and fell asleep by my side, I briefly wondered if I should keep him, but dismissed the thought. I tried it before and it never worked. All my love slaves had outlived their use, became shadows of their former selves in a matter of weeks. Perhaps it was my father's jealous magic that never tolerated any man by my side. Or perhaps it was my own, the magic of the Mistress of the Solstice that drew life and love out of everything living, the magic that taught me the hard way not to keep any mortal bonds.

Besides, I had better things to do. This night with Kirill was all I needed to draw my thoughts away from men for a while, to satisfy the urges of my flesh, to prepare me for another glorious Solstice.

I looked at his sleeping form stretched beside me, and let him go.

I did not bother to collect my dress, still heaped at the foot of his bed. He would wonder when he woke up, but that was not my concern. Let him wonder, and treasure the memory for as long as he chose.

As a dove I flew away into the night air. In my bird form, I flew through the tall grass fields, bathing in the night dew to wash off his sweat and seed, his smell that I did not want to carry with me into the palace. Then I went home.

Anna Kashina

IVAN

"**H**ere," Wolf whispered.

Ivan peered into the moonlit glade. Tall grass shimmered silver in the waning moonlight, blending into the shade of thick firs at the far end. The lake on the other side was barely visible through the tall reed fence that left open only a narrow strip of water, its small black tongues lazily lapping at the muddy bank.

"Keep to the trees," Wolf said. "If he sees your tracks, he won't land."

Ivan held his breath as he crept around the glade toward the water. The gnarled old log loomed out of the grass like a sinking ship, raising its twisted finger-like twigs toward the darkening sky. Careful to leave no tracks, Ivan leaned over the log and spread the thin net over its surprisingly smooth surface. Touching it brought to mind another analogy. Old bones. Ivan hastily withdrew his hand, pausing at the edge of the trees to marvel at the way the Net blended with the wood. Even if he looked very hard, he couldn't see it at all.

A distant shriek brought him back to reality even before he felt Wolf's teeth tugging his shirt. Their sharp pull nearly sent him tumbling over. He dove for the cover, forcing his shallow breath out through his nose, so that no sound would escape. Still, when he finally settled in his shelter of drooping fir branches and looked at the glade again, he nearly cried out in surprise.

The log was no longer empty. A large bird perched on it, so black that its feathers seemed to draw in the moonlight, a pit of darkness from which the dark glistening bead of an eye darted in desperate glances at the lake and the forest ahead.

The eye emanated a light of its own—a deep amber glow that reminded Ivan of the pit of a dying fire.

"Now," Wolf whispered.

"But—" Ivan's voice caught in his throat as he saw Raven glance his way. It seemed impossible that anyone could hear him from this distance. But Raven was an Immortal, and one lesson Ivan had learned well during his travels with Wolf was not to underestimate the Immortals.

Still, he was supposed to come out of hiding only when Raven was caught in the Net. No matter how hard he tried, he could see no trace of the Net on the smooth surface of the log. Nor did Raven behave like he imagined a trapped bird would. No agonized beating against the unbreakable magical bonds. No deadly swipes from a razor-sharp beak. He just sat there, calm, as if taking a rest after a long flight. If anything, he looked bored.

"I said, *go*," Wolf growled.

Startled, Ivan stumbled forward into the opening as if pushed by an invisible hand. He briefly wondered if Wolf had actually used magic, despite his promise never to use it on Ivan. But there was no time, and nothing that Ivan could do as he approached the protruding log through the dew-covered grass.

"Hello," he said shakily.

Raven cocked his head to one side. His bored expression changed to one of amusement.

"I—I—" Ivan stumbled. He knew it wouldn't be easy to trap an Immortal and force him to do his bidding, but this absence of resistance was more unnerving than any fight. "I have you in my power," he said, forcing his voice steady.

Raven shifted on the log, and only then did Ivan notice how he was shuffling his feet, as if they were tethered to the wood. He also imagined he saw a delicate web-like thread glimmer against Raven's wing, but he couldn't be sure. He forced himself not to stare.

"As far as I understand the rules," he said, "you must now do what I say."

A click of a beak sounded too much like a suppressed chuckle. Or did Ivan imagine it?

"Ask away, boy," Raven said. "What is it you want to know?"

Ivan froze. Was he so easy to read, or did Raven already know what Ivan wanted? And if so, did anyone else know too? Ivan suppressed the thought, glancing back into the fir thicket that he knew hid Wolf, the silent observer. Only one could ask questions. He wished bitterly that he didn't have to be the one.

"Why do you think I want information?" he asked cautiously.

The dry eye glistened with amusement as Raven clicked his beak again. Its edges looked sharp, and more powerful than the teeth of a wild beast. Only now, up close, did Ivan realize how much larger Raven was compared to any other raven he had ever seen.

"Because," Raven said, "I know my true worth. I assume you do too, since you went through all this trouble on my account."

It would have been so much easier if Raven looked even a little bit unnerved. As far as Ivan understood, the power of the magic net could trap Raven for eternity, far longer than the span of Ivan's mortal lifetime. But now didn't seem to be a good moment to bring it up. He threw another helpless glance at Wolf's hiding place. How did he agree to end up with the task of questioning Raven?

"Your true worth?" he asked.

This is your quest, Wolf had said. *You'll know what to do.*

Back then, Ivan had been certain he would. Yet now, under the penetrating stare of his captive, he wasn't sure anymore.

This time the sound that escaped Raven's beak seemed more like a snort.

"If you've gone through all the trouble of capturing me and you don't know what you want of me, I pity you, boy."

Ivan took a breath. "I am told this net will hold you captive until you bargain your way out."

Raven gave him a long look. "Those who would bargain must know what they want. Do you?"

Why was this so difficult? Ivan knew what he wanted. Right? He cleared his throat. "Tell me how to get into the East Tower of the Castle."

The amusement in Raven's eyes veiled with pity. "Are you sure this is truly what you want?"

"Yes."

"Easy," Raven said. "Take the path over there. It leads straight to the tower wall. The stones are so beaten that a sleek boy like you can easily climb it. There's only one window on that side, at the second storey. It will take you into a circular room, into the heart of the East Tower. Hardly worth the trouble of capturing me, is it?"

Ivan shook his head. "I'm told there're traps on the way to the wall."

"Oh?" The black eye rolled in its socket. "And who told you that?"

Ivan sighed. "The same person who told me that to gain your freedom, you have to answer all my questions. And that the Net makes it impossible for you to lie."

"A wise person indeed," Raven said thoughtfully. "I only wonder why the very same person couldn't tell you what you need to know and save us both the trouble of this spectacle."

He sounded so much like a grouchy old man, one of those that sit by the well in every village, endlessly chatting about their neighbors. Except that this old man was so different, Ivan reminded himself. Bird form was only a small part of it. He had to watch himself, or Raven could easily trick him to his doom.

"Tell me how to avoid the traps," he said.

"Who told you they can be avoided?"

Ivan met the creature's eyes. "*Can* they be avoided?"

Raven's gaze wavered and lowered to study the specks of moonlight glistening on the drops of dew. The air smelled of night lily, a heady scent that easily went to the head. Ivan inhaled it, wishing that he could be far away from here. If only he could ever find peace.

"Yes, they can be," Raven said at length.

Ivan exhaled slowly, forcing his breath to quiet down. "Then, why didn't you tell me about them in the first place?"

Raven shrugged. "You didn't ask."

"I thought I did."

Raven's dark eyes met his. "Listen, boy, you captured me. But, don't expect me to help you as well. Ask your smart tutors, whoever they are, to get you out of the mess you've gotten yourself into." He closed his beak with a snap and turned away.

Ivan frowned. "I have you in my power! You are bound to answer me."

Raven shrugged. "I have answered your every question, haven't I?"

A retort froze on Ivan's lips. True, Raven had answered every one of his questions. Yet, Ivan hadn't learned anything. Why?

The answer, when it came, seemed so obvious as it taunted Ivan from the shadows of his own mind that he almost laughed out loud.

Ask the right questions, you fool. Ask, and he will answer them, each and every one.

Could it really be this simple?

"Answer me," Ivan said firmly. "What is the first trap?"

There was a pause before the dark shape turned to him again, moving stiffly within the airy bonds of the Net.

"You're not as daft as you look, boy. Now, listen."

MARYA

I landed on the windowsill of my bedroom and folded my dove wings, shaking off the dampness of the night air. My head still swam with memories as I stood before my Mirror, changing back into my normal form. My darkening hair, growing to its normal length. My cheeks, losing their fullness and rosy color. My long black dress, its silky folds caressing my skin, enfolding me down to my bare feet. Kirill would wonder when he woke up and saw my peasant clothes still heaped at the foot of his bed. I smiled at the thought.

There was one more thing I needed to do before I could sleep.

Noiselessly, I took the narrow winding stair from my quarters to the kitchens. The damp, salty smell of boiling meat hit my nostrils. My nose twitched. The Mistress of the Solstice did not eat meat. Yet our castle, like any other royal dwelling, had to feed many mouths. Every day the butchers in the back yard slaughtered a cow to feed our household. The meat was cooked throughout the day and all the bones and unwanted cuts were thrown into a giant pot constantly boiling on the stove. The thick soup it became, called '*varevo*', was the late-night favorite of the tired kitchen staff.

The meaty smell of *varevo* made my stomach turn. I hadn't eaten since morning, before I'd embarked on my journey to the Pine Village. It seemed ages ago. I swayed and clasped the wall until my balance returned, before proceeding deeper into the warm belly of the kitchen, its very stones saturated with the smell of food.

I caught a movement out of the corner of my eye and froze.

The side door creaked open and torchlight hit my face.

"Mistress?" The voice was more frightened than surprised.

"Pavel?" I guessed, straining to see against the blaze.

He lowered the torch and hesitantly stepped forward. Despite his height of almost a *sazhen*, his fear made him look small.

The commoners believed I brought bad luck. While understandable in the villages, I thought the superstition surprising for the inhabitants of the palace. Yet, many of them were born in villages and raised by old wives. Solstice legends of the loveless, love-free Mistress who hunted for virgins on Midsummer eve traveled far across the lands. Except for Prazkovia and my handmaids, everyone in the castle took care to keep their distance.

"I—um—was out late, t'tend to the horses. It's mighty chilly out there. Klava told me there's some *varevo* left. Er—forgive me, Mistress, for disturbin' you."

He edged back into the doorway. He looked so miserable that I almost smiled.

"Go on, Pavel," I said. "You won't disturb me. My business here is short."

He nodded. "Should'n ye wan' that I shine some light for ye, Mistress?" he asked. "It's mighty dark n'there."

"I'll be fine," I assured him. It felt strange to talk to the stableman. I never saw the servants up close. I could smell hay and horse sweat on him, and fancied I saw callouses on his rough hands.

I found my way into the small storeroom, a heady smell of herbs guiding my way. Moonlight from a narrow window faintly illuminated the rows of jars on the shelves and the bundles hanging from the ceiling.

Moving by habit rather than by sight, I picked out nine herbs, breaking a bit off each bundle and putting them into the mug I found on the shelf. By the end of it, my head was swimming and I could no longer tell the smell of one herb from another.

Feeling my way in the dark, I brought my trophies back into the kitchen. At the far table, Pavel loomed over a bowl of *varevo*. He was dipping a chunk of bread into the thick meat broth and smacking his lips with a dreamy expression. I regretted for a moment that I could not enjoy simple food the way he did.

As I made my way into another part of the kitchen, where the smaller kettle with water for tea still hung over the hot embers, a shape blocked my way. I paused, making out the features of a plump woman, her head wrapped in a gray woolen scarf.

"Klava?" I asked. "What are you doing up?"

"Mistress," she said with firm respect. "I am under Praskovia's orders."

"Oh." I stepped back, glad I could still feel amused and not merely angry. "And what would those orders be?"

"Well," Klava took a deep breath, obviously gathering her courage, "Praskovoia—she said you didn't send for your herb drink tonight, and that you haven't eaten since morning. She said you'd come for the drink for sure and that I ought to catch you when you do and give you some borscht. She said it's no good for you to go hungry, with all the important work you do for us all, and you are already so thin—" she paused, sensing with a good servant's instinct that she was about to go too far.

Praskovia. I should have realized she'd notice my absence. She knew of my adventures and never offered any judgment, as long as I was well fed and cared for. I should have sent for my herb drink before I went out. Was I really so affected by my encounter of the afternoon?

Weariness swept over me. I had no energy left to pour hot water into my brew. I had no energy to make my way up the stone steps to the top of the East Tower. It suddenly seemed so desirable to have this plump, kind-faced woman take care of me.

"Very well," I said, handing her the mug. "You can make the brew for me yourself. And, I will eat just a little borscht."

I walked past the stunned cook's helper and sank onto the stone bench across the table from Pavel. The stableman almost choked on his bread. His large hands clenched the edge of his bowl and again, despite his size, he looked small.

"Relax, Pavel," I smiled to him. "I don't bite."

"Right ye are, Mistress," he mumbled and hurriedly finished his meal.

The borscht was delicious. No one besides our cook could achieve such a deep beet-red color that, as you mixed in the sour cream, turned into golden orange, shiny droplets of oil suspended among the vegetable slices. My borscht was made special, without meat, yet rich enough to replenish my strength. As I finished the generous bowl and washed it down with my aromatic herbal brew, I felt my exhaustion turn into the normal tiredness after a well spent day. I made my way up to my room and fell asleep as soon as my head touched the pillow.

IVAN

Ivan remembered. He'd lain near death, before this all started.

He'd heard voices through the daze of his sickness. He hadn't even known if they were real.

"You still have your touch, old man," said a raspy voice with a low timbre that made Ivan's hair stand on end. The rasp seemed to be there entirely for the purpose of smothering the force the voice emanated.

For a brief moment it sounded pleased.

"Do you really think he's the one?" replied a more ordinary voice.

The rasp turned into a rumble. "There's no such thing as 'the one'. Humans invent these tales to give purpose to their miserable existence."

"So, why him?" the other pressed.

There was a pause. "I sense strength in him. That look in his eyes—"

"But he's just a boy," objected the other. There were more notes in the voice now. It wasn't really ordinary, Ivan realized. It had only seemed ordinary next to the force of its companion.

"He cannot even fight."

"There have been fighters in the past. And where did all the fighting get them?"

"But this one—he's like a child."

"Exactly. Have you looked into his eyes? I mean, really *looked*? He's not afraid of anything."

Again, there was a pause. Then the other voice said, "And you think it is enough?"

This time the rumble resembled a roar. Ivan had strained to open his eyes to see the owner of the voice, but he couldn't move. He wasn't even certain he wasn't dreaming.

"You humans invent all sorts of hardships to hide your fear. So, where a regular man would dwell on those non-existent hardships and falter, a fearless one may walk right through the obstacles without seeing them."

There was a longer pause this time. Then, the other voice responded quietly. "There's no such thing as a fearless man."

"Perhaps not," the raspy voice said. "But this one fits."

"Fits what?"

"Everything. All the petty details you humans invented. Even the birthmark."

"Oh, come now, isn't that a bit of a stretch?"

"The timing's right, too. It is the Rule of Immortals, isn't it?"

"It has been for the past four hundred years. And it will be, for ages to come. Kashchey is nearly immortal himself."

"Undead."

"Undead, then. In any case, he isn't going anywhere soon. It should give us some time to find someone better than this boy."

"I tell you, he's the right one. I can feel it. Trust the old creature."

"But his wounds—"

"Just bring him back, Nikifor. Leave the rest to me."

Nikifor. Straining to remember where he had heard the name before, Ivan had sunk back into his death-like sleep.

Nikifor. The old man with white hair and the serene look in his eyes. Ivan had never learned the meaning of the strange conversation he'd half-heard, half-dreamed as he lay on death's doorstep struggling to come back to the living.

He slowly shook his head, coming back from the world of memory.

Something caught his eye in the last beams of the setting

moon. He bent down and carefully picked a flower out of the thick grass. It was a common flower, an inflorescence of purple-and-yellow that shone like a tiny star in the greenery of the meadow. The purple was actually the leaves, each wrapping a delicate yellow flower in a lover's embrace. But to an untrained eye they looked like two kinds of flowers on one stem. To reflect this duality, people had given the flower a double name. *Ivan-and-Marya.*

"Picking flowers, lad?" Wolf asked. "I thought we were in a hurry."

Ivan lowered his eyes. "I—"

"Oh, don't let me disturb you!" Wolf growled as he stretched the words. "It's still a few hours before dawn. Plenty of time. Glad we didn't have to go through any trouble to get here in the first place."

Ivan tucked the flower into his shirt. "Is this why Gleb was so surprised to hear my name?"

"Ivan and Marya are the two most common names in these parts. *That* is why the villagers gave the flower such a name. You know it as well as I do."

"Yes, but what if—"

"If what?"

Ivan sighed. "Don't you believe in destiny?"

There was a sound an untrained ear could mistake for sneezing as the wolf hastily turned away.

"Did I say something funny?"

"No," Wolf growled. "I'm just laughing at myself. After all these centuries I had to be stupid enough to entrust a serious task to a silly human boy."

"You think I'll fall in love with her?"

Wolf shrugged. "Everyone else does. Gleb tried to tell you, not that you really listened, of course."

"I am not in love!" Ivan protested. "It would be utterly stupid to fall in love with someone who kills people in cold blood. Even more stupid to fall in love with someone you've never really met."

"Exactly my point." Wolf nodded. "Exactly my point."

Ivan turned toward the looming castle wall. Wolf trotted beside him. Sometimes he looked just like a dog—a monstrous one whose head reached almost to a man's shoulder, but a dog nonetheless.

"Just remember everything we learned," Wolf said. "Try not to trigger the traps. Once you're inside, go straight for the box. Make sure you don't get distracted with anything else, you hear me?"

"Mmm," Ivan said.

"Hey, boy! Are you still with me?"

"I thought if I could just talk to her—"

Wolf sighed. "You already did, remember? Back on the plaza? If you forgot, look at your arm. I'm sure it couldn't have healed this quickly."

"But out there I had no time to really say anything! If I could only reason with her—"

"Yes, right." Wolf skirted a rowan branch that hung low over the path. "She'll take one look at you, forget all about her duties, and run off with you to your Twelfth Kingdom. Quite a reasonable thing to do, considering her situation."

Dejected, Ivan walked for a while in silence. "What her father makes her do is wrong. She must see it too."

"I'm sure she does," Wolf agreed.

There was another pause.

"There isn't much risk in trying," Ivan finally said.

"No risk at all. She's a sorceress, true, but she isn't generally known for blowing people's heads off. She leaves that task to her father. Who might do just that, if he happens to come to her chambers during your little conversation—"

"In the middle of the night?"

"Marya and her father have a very close relationship," Wolf replied pointedly.

"Well," Ivan hesitated, "if worst comes to worst, I could always ask for her hand in marriage."

Wolf stared. "Oh, is that what this is all about, boy? Why ever didn't you tell me?"

"It's not that," Ivan blushed so deeply that his pale face

71

turned dark in the waning light. "It's just that if I do, then, by the rules, neither she nor Kashchey could hurt me."

"Did Gleb tell you this?"

"Yes, when you were out. He said the rule is as strict as the code of the Immortals. He said Kashchey won't harm me if I call upon the rule, especially because he tries so hard to be known as a real Immortal himself."

"Your charms must be going to your head, lover boy. You forget, you're not a Tzar's son anymore. You're no match for her. Not in this kingdom."

"I know," Ivan said slowly. "But I don't think it matters. Anyone can be a suitor if they fulfill her task."

"Did Gleb by any chance mention that if you fail at her task, then, by law of this kingdom you must die?"

Ivan's face lost some of its dreamy expression.

"Yes, he did, but I'm only talking about it as a way to retreat. If the situation becomes dangerous."

"In case you haven't noticed," Wolf growled. "Despite the swarm of suitors that are drawn to this kingdom like flies to honey, she is still unwed. Any thoughts why? Don't you forget this, boy. Marya and her father, Kashchey, aren't as easy as old Leshy. They play no games."

Ivan eyed him uncertainly.

"Just do what I tell you. Your only true advantage is surprise. Get in, grab the Needle and run for your life. Don't even think of casting an eye on her."

They stopped in sight of a large, gnarled oak, its deformed roots jutting out of the ground, twisting toward them like enormous fingers. In the waning moonlight, Ivan imagined he could see the glimmer of the web stretched across the path. But it was only his imagination. The web couldn't possibly be visible from this distance.

"It looks like I can go no further," Wolf said. "Only one can pass. You're on your own, boy."

Ivan nodded. He couldn't fail. Not after everything they'd gone through.

"Remember everything the old bird told you, boy," Wolf

said. Then he padded back into the shelter of the trees.

Ivan carefully approached the large oak. When he was twenty paces away, he crouched and crept forward until he could see the shimmering silver of the water droplets hanging across the path. They were so thin that if Ivan hadn't known to look for them, he would have walked right into them without noticing.

It all seemed so easy when Raven had told him. He could still hear the bird's voice in his head—at least he did until Wolf shouted at him afterwards for releasing their prisoner. But Ivan knew he could never focus on his task if he had left Raven trapped and helpless back on that log. Despite how thin and airy it was, the Net had rendered him nearly immobile. Powerful magical objects could be truly frightening.

But now, standing in front of the first trap, he bitterly wished Raven was here. Or at least that he could go back to ask again.

A magical mist that must be unraveled, if one wished to follow the path to the castle. It could be unraveled, Raven said, if you found the right droplet. But touch the wrong one—and the mist would trap you, rob you of your mind and send you into the swamp.

Ivan swallowed, looking at the dark, glistening water at the side of the path. It glimmered like a giant eye, winking at him invitingly. Was this entire kingdom built on swamps?

He strained his eyes to make out the delicate meshwork of silvery beads. "Imagine a net that holds them in place," Raven had said. "An invisible net, much like the one that traps me now. It goes in a spiral, from the center outward. You must find the outmost droplet and follow them in, one at a time."

Easier said than done.

Ivan lowered his head, trying to find a position from which the glimmer of the water droplets caught the moonlight. They glistened like precious jewels, their radiating beauty, magnified by the magic that powered it.

There. Did he see a dark line, cutting through the magical glimmer?

"It's imaginary," Raven had said. "But you must see it as if it is real. Once you touch the first droplet, you must not stop."

Ivan carefully reached forward toward the lone droplet on the outer rim of the water circle.

He imagined more than heard a barely perceptible popping sound, and a sudden chill in his fingertip, like a prickle of a cold needle. He kept his hand steady as he moved it along the droplet path, straining to maintain the image of the invisible spiral in his mind. There. The last droplet.

A sigh rustled through the grass under his feet and rippled the swamp water at the side of the path. Ivan straightened and exhaled a breath he was holding. He hadn't realized how numb his arm became from the strain of keeping it steady.

He shakily got up to his feet, watching the last bits of the mist disappear into the swamp. So much for the first trap. That wasn't so hard, was it?

At least, he was still alive.

He steadied himself. His hand felt numb, his tingling fingers slowly coming back to life. Taking a deep breath, he followed the path further to the castle wall.

Heat hit his face without warning, the path in front of him erupting into fire. Ivan froze in his tracks. He almost let his relief carry him straight into the next trap. Not that he could do anything to stop it.

Raven did not warn him it would come so soon.

The narrow path in front of him was an inferno, the fire consuming it left and right, straight to the edges of the swamp water now spreading on both sides. Ivan could feel the heat biting into his skin, dissolving the last bits of the numbness caused by the magical mist. The fire was slowly approaching, its fiery tongues snaking along the path toward his feet.

"Whatever you do, don't turn back," Raven had told him. "You would want to turn and run away, but as soon as you do, the fire will consume you. This is why most of the suitors who try to brave the East Tower leave no trace behind."

Ivan shivered. The old bird seemed to take pleasure in telling him those details. Now that he was facing the trap, the knowledge of what would happen to him if he failed didn't help one bit.

He carefully breathed in. The air stung and his insides protested at the sudden pain. *Don't move. Don't. Move.*

The fire was upon him. He could see its red tongues raging around him, licking his skin. He felt his skin emanate hissing sounds as it bubbled and burst, running down his exposed flesh. His eyes hurt, but closing them did not help, for the fire reached up to his face, singing his hair, peeling away his eyelids. The pain was impossible. He had never felt anything like it.

He knew he shouldn't scream, but what really stopped him was no longer any conscious knowledge but the fact that screaming required breathing in, and he knew his smoldering lungs could possibly take no more. Yet, if he failed to breathe, he would die.

Assuming it mattered.

Raven had said that if he withstood this trial he wouldn't be harmed, but that didn't seem to matter either, for how could he live much longer without skin, with the smoldering flesh rapidly withering in the unbearable heat. He could *smell* it, a sickening smell of roasting meat that made the bile rise into his throat. But he couldn't vomit either. He had no breath left.

Good bye, Wolf. Forgive me for failing.

And then, just as suddenly, it was over. The heat dissipated, leaving behind a cool breath of the night air. It carried the damp chill of the swamp, so welcome on his burning skin.

His skin.

It couldn't possibly be there, could it?

How could he possibly have lived through that?

He counted under his breath and slowly opened his eyes.

The path in front of him was clear, tall grass on either side glimmering in the scarce light from the nigh sky. It wavered in the breeze, parting before his feet into the thin, scantly trodden path he had been following.

It did not look as if it had been touched by fire at all.

Ivan took a deep breath, enjoying the cool relief it brought to his tortured insides. He breathed some more, letting his muscles unknot before he dared to lift his hands up to his eyes to survey the damage.

His skin was all there, smooth and white, calloused at the fingertips. Ivan sighed. He shouldn't be surprised, he knew. Raven told him this would happen. Yet, after being consumed by the fire, it was hard to imagine how he could still feel so whole.

Too much. This had been too much. How could he possibly go on?

He took another step along the path. Then another.

Don't stop. Not when you are so close.

His feet carried him forward, first slowly, then faster as he finally saw the roughly hewn wall looming ahead. It was so close he could see the cracks in the moss-covered stones, perfect footholds for someone trying to climb up. Nothing to it, just like Raven said.

A dark winged shape swept overhead. Ivan dropped to the ground and rolled over, barely avoiding the sweep of the razor-sharp claws. *Focus, you fool. The last trap.*

Too late, he remember Raven's warning. "Stop, as soon as you see the wall. Don't take another step before you see the creature."

Had he messed it up?

His silent attacker circled and returned for another pass. Crouching, Ivan reached for his dagger. "Don't fight it," Raven had said. "Don't even try. You cannot possibly win. Above all, *don't look at it.*" The warning echoed in Ivan's ears just in time as he was about to turn his head. If only the damned thing would make more sound. How was he supposed to resist if he couldn't even look at it?

How could he possibly survive its attack if he couldn't fight back?

The sweep of air at the back of his neck was his only warning. He was too slow this time. A sharp claw grazed his shoulder, biting deep into the skin. He forced back a cry as he rolled over the ground again, this time in the right direction. Toward the water. Here.

The dark gleaming swamp puddle at the foot of the castle reflected the moonless sky, the tower at his back looming over it like a cliff. He could see the movement over it as the creature swept down again. Dear gods. So huge. It could probably kill him with a single strike. And now that it drew blood—

He held still, bracing for his next move. He could see the creature at his back growing in size as it advanced, impossibly fast. Claws, bigger than Wolf's, gleamed on its paws, raised for a strike. Silver-white eyes focused on him with cold precision. Dear gods.

The creature's face was that of a woman, beautiful and calm, like the treacherous swamp waters. It had breasts, naked and full, their skin gleaming white as they swelled at the base of her long, slender neck. The rest of the body was covered with fur, the creature's bear limbs and bat-like wings a terrifying contrast with the cold beauty of its face.

Frozen in fascination, Ivan nearly forgot to move in time. At the last minute, he dove out of the creature's way.

It recovered, beating its enormous wings, raising the wind in their wake. But this small delay was enough. Ivan was ready this time as he shot out his hand and splashed water from his flask over the flying creature.

He expected more, a hiss, or perhaps a scream. Instead, the creature just dissipated, like a wisp of black smoke from a dying stove.

Once again, the air was clear, the night cold and still, as if nothing had happened here before.

Trembling, Ivan sank to the grass. He did it. He had bested all of the Mistress's traps. Now all he had to do was climb up and claim his prize.

He looked up the rough, moss-covered stone wall.

He was not sure he had enough strength left to do it.

Anna Kashina

MARYA

That night, I had the dream again. I was walking through the forest, clenching something in my hand. Something oval and warm to the touch. I wanted to open my hand and look, but the force of the dream drew me forward to the hedge that glistened with sunlight from beyond the distant tree trunks.

It was hard to reach the hedge. My feet sunk deep into the forest floor. Raspberry brambles grabbed at my clothes, holding me back with their sticky hands. Hazelnut bushes slapped me in the face. Young fir trees tried to prick me through the thin cloth of my dress. But I was persistent. I knew I had to reach the hedge and step out into the sunlight.

As always in my dream, as I finally tore free from the forest's clutches, I found myself in the glade next to the Sacrifice Pool. In the very same place where each year a chosen maiden submerged into the water to be swallowed forever by Kupalo's love and my father's need.

A man was waiting for me in the glade. A dark man crouching by the water. As I stepped out of the forest and saw him, fear engulfed me. I knew the man was about to turn his head and I was desperately afraid to see his face. As I saw his muscles tense and his head begin to turn, I screamed.

And woke up.

I sat up in bed, my heart beating, my eyes slowly adjusting to the darkness from the bright sunlight of the glade in my dream. I was alone in my room. It was night. There was no strange man. Everything was well.

And then I saw a shape by the window.

A man.

Horrified, I watched him step from the shadows toward

me, slowly coming into view. In the dim light I watched his face, his straw hair, his eyes smiling at me with such gentleness that my heart nearly stopped beating in fear of scaring it away. He stopped in front of me, looking straight into my eyes.

"Hello, Marya Tzarevna," he said, and the sound of his voice made me shiver.

Except, strangely, my fear was gone.

Holding my gaze, he stepped forward and lowered to a crouch beside my bed, so that his face was level with mine. Warmth tingled in my awakening body. I suddenly felt easy, as if the sun has come out from behind a cloud. He smiled and I suppressed the urge to smile back.

"You are even more beautiful than I remember," he said quietly. It was a statement, not a question or an invitation to speak. So I continued to look at him, feeling my body slowly warm under his gaze.

I should have called the guards. There was an intruder in my bedroom at night. Yet, I could not imagine any danger coming from this harmless looking boy. After the terror of my nightmare I wanted to enjoy the feeling of calm he emanated, if only for a moment.

I suddenly became aware that I was naked under the covers and pulled my blanket up to my neck. He drew back and, searching around with his eyes, found my dress, thrown over the back of the chair. He picked it up and handed it to me. It seemed natural, like a child's game. I pulled the dress over my head and stood up, straightening it out.

And came to my full senses.

I was alone with a man, who had obviously overcome all my deadly traps to come to my bedroom at night.

"How did you get here?" I demanded.

"I climbed up the wall," he said. "It isn't all that hard."

Trying to appear calm, I lit a candle in a sconce on the wall and in its reddish flickering light I looked him up and down. He hadn't been killed by my traps, which in itself seemed unbelievable, but he should at least look badly beaten. My father and I believed the traps impossible to avoid.

I could see no significant signs of hardship in his neat clothing. He still wore a peasant's garb, but it was different from what he'd worn on the palace plaza. His fine linen shirt was embroidered with a thread at the neck. It was ripped below the shoulder, a dark splotch spreading around the gash. Blood? My skin tingled at this new evidence that he was speaking the truth. He *did* encounter, and apparently overcome, my traps. But how?...

I continued my inspection. His dark baggy pants and the *lapti* on his feet looked new, perhaps a bit grass-stained. I could see the strong line of his neck running into the wide opening of the shirt, the muscle of his arms, the width of his shoulders under the bleached fabric. He bore no visible weapon, only a short dagger on his belt, but his body was lean and fit like a warrior's.

I forced thoughts of his body away. They hardly seemed to fit the occasion.

"Listen," I said. "I don't know who you are..."

"I am Ivan, the youngest son of Tzar Erofei of the Twelfth Kingdom," he answered readily. Then he paused and added with a quick smile: "I'm also known as Ivan the Fool."

His smile was so hard to resist. I lowered my eyes to suppress an unseemly desire to giggle. He made me feel carefree, the way I hadn't felt in years.

"The fool," I said. "Indeed."

Names. How did it happen that he told me his name?

Names were like bonds. They made things personal. They made people feel as if they knew each other.

They made people care.

They made it so much harder to do what was right.

I shook the feeling off. There would be time to deal with it later, or so I hoped.

His gaze held me. The blue of his eyes was like a lure, a promise of a life I could never have, the call of a distant heavenly land. If I had been born a simple village maiden, if I didn't bear my gruesome duty of conducting an annual sacrifice, if I was free to love—

I forced myself back to my senses.

Love. One did not speak of the enemy on the verge of the Solstice. This word had no place in my thoughts. It was not only forbidden for me, but more, I never desired it. There wasn't a man born who could possibly be my match. Was there?

This boy must be a sorcerer, for no regular mortal could ever make me feel this way.

I drew myself up. "I will give you exactly three seconds to get out of here, Ivan the Fool. If you are not out by then—"

I expected him to spring into action. At the very least, to show some reaction to my words. Instead, he reached into his shirt and pulled out a slightly crumpled purple-and-yellow flower.

"I brought this for you," he said, his face shining with the mischief of a child letting his playmate in on a secret.

In my surprise, I reached out to take it before the realization of what it was hit me full in the face.

These were not two flowers, a purple and yellow, as I'd first thought. This was a single plant, one of the most common in the nearby forests.

Ivan-and-Marya.

My outstretched hand wavered and the flower slipped to the floor.

"Do you believe in destiny, Marya?" he asked softly.

Destiny. Perhaps I was still dreaming, and all this was a figment of my imagination? Perhaps if I indulged in this, just a moment longer, there would be no harm? Wasn't I allowed to have a pleasant dream every once in a while?

I slowly looked up to meet his eyes.

"There's no such thing as destiny," I said.

He reached over and took my hand.

I melted into his touch like cream melts into hot bread, like a drop of ice melts into a patch of spring sunlight. The warmth of his skin, the brush of his fingers against mine echoed through my body with a shudder so strong it shook me to my very soul.

I had known the touch of many men. I didn't even care to remember how many. But not like this.

I felt naked under his gentle gaze. I swayed with the slightest movement of the night air. The soles of my feet were burned by the smooth stone floor. I was transparent to the warmth of his gaze, the sunlight of his smile.

His touch.

And then he spoke, his soft voice caressing me like a breath of warm wind.

"I am the happiest man in the world to be able to see you so close. You are beautiful beyond belief."

I forced a smile. "Don't you know? I am the most beautiful woman in the world."

"You are, indeed!" he exclaimed. "And, yet, no legend could do you justice." He stepped closer, and I inhaled his smell, sun-baked grass and fresh river water. It made my head spin.

No man I had known ever smelled like this. I allowed myself a moment to revel in his smell, resisting the urge to step forward and sink into his arms.

If I wanted to remain sane, I had to stop this right now.

It was time to wake up.

I pulled my hand out of his hold and drew away. A breath of the cool night air with the familiar smells of stone and dry wood settled over my confused senses.

"If you don't leave this instant—"

"I need to talk to you, Marya," he said. "That's why I am here."

"Talk to me? What about?"

"The Solstice."

Now that I kept my distance from him it was easier to stay sane. In the dim light I could no longer see his eyes, shrouded in deep shadow, nor catch his scent, carried away by the draft at my back. It was easier to concentrate.

"What in particular do you wish to know about the Solstice?"

His neck became tense, a barely perceptible change that made me instantly alert.

"Do you know why your father, Kashchey, demands Solstice sacrifice?"

"Not that it's any of your business, since you're obviously an outsider," I said, "but if you must know, it feeds his power to keep our kingdom safe,"

Ivan shook his head, stepping around me so I was forced to turn toward the light.

"It does feed his power," he said. "But this has nothing to do with the good of the kingdom. Those poor girls die to keep him young. They give their lives for his enjoyment. And you have the power to stop this."

I felt my skin tingle as my magic power awoke inside me. "You know nothing about this, Fool. Leave, before I smash you where you stand!"

He didn't move, but I saw the shadows shift on his face as his gaze softened. "You're wrong, Marya," he said quietly. "Deep inside, you know it. Your father keeps you in his power. He controls you. I can help you break free."

A surge of power rushed to my fingertips as I raised my hands, palms out. "Be gone!"

He shook his head and took a step forward.

I lifted my chin. "Since you obviously don't understand words—" Fire crackled in my hands. "Good bye, Fool."

He leapt out of the way of the blast, his movement so quick and fluid that I couldn't help but gape. Had he been tricking me all this time? Was he a great warrior after all?

"Please, Marya," he pleaded. "All I want is talk."

"You've talked enough."

The lack of fear on his face was hypnotizing, but not nearly as unsettling as the touch of pity he continued to look at me. He showed no move to run away. He just stood there, waiting for my next blast. And it was then, as I gathered all my energy to smite him to dust, that I realized that this act would kill me too, that I simply could not bear the thought of putting out the sunlight that emanated from his eyes. Not like this.

I lowered my hands.

"Leave."

"No." He took another step toward me.

My voice sank to a whisper. "Please. I am letting you go. Run, before I change my mind."

"Come with me." He reached over, and I felt my head spin as I realized that he would touch me again, and that if I felt again the warmth of his hand, his smell, I would not be able to resist him anymore. I shrank away from him as if he was a snake.

He took another step. I stared at him, mesmerized. His eyes. His touch—

And then his muscles went tense again as he spun around even before I saw the movement out of the corner of my eye.

Relief and regret washed over me as the stately, black-clad figure crossed the room in a few surefooted strides. His eyes burned like coals in a pale face framed by long dark hair.

My father, Kashchey the Immortal.

IVΛN

Once he saw her up close, there was no going back. He was doomed, and he knew it. Or perhaps the same doom had engulfed both of them, throwing them into a turmoil from which there could be no escape.

She was so much more beautiful up close. And more. She was his soul mate, a true part of him whose closeness was the only thing that could make him feel complete. And she was trapped, helpless and powerful all at the same time, an impossible combination that made him want to stay by her side for the rest of his life, to look into her eyes, to cherish and protect her as she deserved, as she was born to be.

Not to use her, like her father had been. She was so much more than an exquisite tool to quench his dark, vile need.

And then Ivan realized it. His true quest was not to save this year's virgin, and every other virgin to come in her wake. His true quest was to save Marya, Mistress of the Solstice.

When he came to this kingdom, he had been committed to fulfill his quest or die. But now he knew: his soul would not rest until his quest was accomplished.

If he failed, death would not absolve him.

His soul would be destroyed too.

MARYA

My father strode into the room keeping his eyes on Ivan, who stood so still that he seemed like an exquisitely carved statue. I hurried over to Father's side, trembling with the released tension.

I had no idea how much this encounter had drained me.

"Who is this?" my father demanded.

"He calls himself Ivan, Father. A tzar's son from the Twelfth Kingdom. He seems daft, and he is nicknamed a fool. Or so he told me."

"He *is* a fool," my father agreed. "Only fools allow themselves to get tangled in matters they don't understand. Tell me, who is pulling your strings, puppet boy?"

A question formed on my lips, but I didn't have time to voice it, because at that moment Ivan the Fool darted sideways, to the place on the shelf where stood my sewing box and inside it—

The Needle. My father's Death.

As if dreaming, I saw a long narrow streak of silver gleam in the boy's fingers.

"Stay where you are, Kashchey!" Ivan's words rang like a bell through the deadly- still room.

My father turned to me slowly, pale like moonlight. "You told him, Marya! You *betrayed* me!"

The unfairness of it made me gasp. "I didn't."

It didn't matter now. This was my fault. Because of me. Because I hesitated when I should have killed this intruder on the spot. And now, he threatened my father, my world, everything I held dear.

Through the weakness that enfolded me, I continued to

watch the scene unfold

"I could kill you right now, Kashchey." Ivan's voice was quiet, almost friendly.

"I doubt it," my father said calmly. "Only an Immortal can break the Needle. You don't look like an Immortal to me. But in a moment we'll know for sure." He raised his hands.

Ivan held the Needle out in front of his body, in the way of the upcoming blast.

My father hesitated. "It would seem, boy, that you have come here to play with things you don't understand. Why don't you hand the Needle back? I'd hate for it to get lost in what's left of you when I'm done."

Ivan the Fool showed no emotion. Despite his youth, despite his plain clothes, he looked almost like a worthy foe.

What *was* he?

"I will give it back," he said after a pause. "If you promise to give up the Solstice Sacrifice."

My father shrugged and raised his hands again. "Have it your way, fool."

"Wait!" Ivan held out his hand in a halting gesture. Then he turned to me. "There is a rumor, that you, Marya Kashcheevna, grant everyone who seeks your hand a task to fulfill."

"Seeks my hand?" I whispered, briefly meeting my father's gaze. I shivered. Great Kupalo, I had no strength for this anymore.

"I ask for your hand in marriage, Marya Tzarevna," Ivan said solemnly. "I ask you to consider me a suitor and give me a task to fulfill in your name, so that I might gain the sacred honor of calling you mine."

I stared. The rule that any suitor of mine was immune from us until he failed in his task was known only to a few. This secret was guarded even closer than that of the Needle and Raven's Bane, the magic net.

How could this fool have known? Perhaps he was in possession of magic that went beyond my father's skill?

I couldn't imagine such a powerful magic hiding behind

those innocent eyes, that childlike smile, or the disturbing tenderness in his gaze when he looked at me.

I drew myself up.

"You must have also heard, Ivan Tzarevich, that no one has ever returned alive from such a task."

He bowed. "I will do whatever you ask of me, Marya, or die trying."

"Very well." I drew a deep breath. "The Solstice is in twelve days. If you bring me the Water of Life from the Hidden Stream by the Solstice night, I will consider your claim."

I invented these tasks easily when the time came. Sometimes I amused myself by making them seem easy, almost attainable, but this time I took no chances. Hidden Stream was half the world away from our kingdom. Even my Midnight, surely the fastest horse in the world, would require months at a full gallop, assuming he could go without rest. More than that, if by some miracle Ivan the Fool found himself in the right place at the right time, he would still have to make the Hidden Stream reveal itself and give up at least a drop of its water. The Hidden Stream only revealed itself to an Immortal, yet its water was deadly for them, so no Immortal ever ventured out to look for it.

Indeed, I was giving this fool from the Twelfth Kingdom no chance at all.

"Very good, Marya," my father said. Then he turned to Ivan. "Do as my daughter wishes. Give me the Needle and go."

But Ivan was already slipping the Needle into a pouch at his belt, his eyes shining again with that mischief. "I need some security, Kashchey. But I'll keep the Needle safe until I return, you have my word. Farewell, Tzarevna Marya Kashcheevna. See you in twelve days." He bowed gallantly and, jumping over the windowsill, disappeared.

I turned to my father, but he averted his eyes, and I let my hand fall to my side.

"I didn't tell him, Father. Please, believe me."

He didn't respond.

"I'll get the Needle back. I promise."

My father never looked at me. Turning, he strode out of the room.

IVAN

"**Y**ou *what*?" Wolf's eyes glowed like two hot coals.

"I asked for her hand."

Wolf sat down on the ground and scratched his ear in a dog-like gesture.

Ivan waited, making sure to stay out of the way of the flying bits of fur. Wolf always calmed down. Eventually.

"Do you mean you couldn't find the Needle in time? It wasn't in the box?"

"It was in the box. I found it at once." Ivan lowered his head waiting for a further outburst. Nothing happened. After a while he dared a look. Wolf's eyes were so close to his that he had to hold himself from jumping back in fear. The old beast could move like a ghost. When angered, he was much more frightening than Kashchey and Leshy together.

"Then, what happened?" Wolf snarled. "All you needed was to grab the Needle and get out of there. How hard could it be?"

"I do have the Needle," Ivan said. "Here." He fumbled in the pouch at his belt. His hands shook. He had never seen Wolf like this.

"Keep it," Wolf said. "It can't be used unless you fulfill your suitor's task."

He turned and walked away along the forest path.

"Wait!" Ivan called out. When no answer came, he started along the path after the disappearing gray tail, first at a walk, then at a run. "Please, don't leave!"

"You have a task to fulfill," Wolf said without turning. "Go, do it. If you survive you'll get yourself a lovely bride. Deadly, true. But quite a beauty. Skillful in bed, too, that's what I heard. Maybe she'll teach you a thing or two about love."

"Don't you want to know what the task is?" Ivan panted. He could fall in rhythm with the wolf's slow trot, but talking on the run was hard.

"Why? I'm not the one who got himself into this mess. And, whatever task she gave you, you're meat, boy. I'd be better off finding myself another hero. A real one, this time." Wolf spat out the last words before speeding up.

Ivan strained to match his pace.

"We have twelve days before the Solstice," he gasped. "We could still make it."

"I said forget it, boy."

"I am sorry," Ivan said between breaths. "I really am. I hesitated up there. I—I lost my chance."

There was no answer, but after a while Wolf started to slow down, eventually falling into a walk. Ivan hurried along, struggling to steady his breath.

"D'you know what it takes to fulfill a prophecy?" Wolf said after a while. "There are times you can't hesitate."

"Look," Ivan pleaded, "can we please slow down to discuss it? I can't keep up much longer."

"You can never keep up." Yet, after a few more paces Wolf stopped and faced Ivan. "All right, boy, I'll hear you out."

The house looked deserted. The shutters swung on broken hinges. From behind them, the dark empty windows gaped like the eyes of a blind man. The wicker fence was broken in so many places it hardly looked like a fence anymore, and the small path from the gate to the house's front door was overgrown with tall weeds, among which the jagged leaves of the stinging nettle reached out in a vain attempt to catch a trespasser unawares.

There were no trespassers here. Who would trespass in this desolate place?

"What're we waiting for?"

"Hush." Wolf peered into the dusk.

"Why?" Ivan whispered after a long silence.

"Do you know the saying: 'Don't wake the trouble'—?"

"You mean, 'don't *trouble* the trouble'?"

"Whatever you humans say."

"What trouble?" The words froze on Ivan's lips.

The door of the house swung open with a creak that was carried on the wind like a human wail. And then it slammed shut by itself. There was a thud, then a rustle as something invisible made its way through the weeds to the gate in the fence. The gate opened and closed. Then everything went quiet again.

Ivan felt chills creep up his spine.

"Now," Wolf said.

"What was that?" Ivan whispered.

"I said, *now*, boy." Wolf's rumbling whisper echoed in Ivan's gut. It was not a pleasant sensation.

Crouching, he followed Wolf to the house.

Wolf paused by the door. "Don't make me do it, boy," he growled. "Open the door."

"What is this place?" Ivan asked. He hesitated to touch the crooked wooden doorknob.

"Trouble. It lives here. Now, get inside before someone sees you!"

Ivan took a deep breath and pulled the door. It moaned as if alive. Trying not to think of what was waiting for them inside, Ivan followed Wolf's gray shape into the darkness. The door shut behind them with a thud, and Ivan wondered if they'd be able to get out.

As he stepped from the entry way into the room, he realized that it was not as dark as he'd feared. Light from the rising moon streamed through the window, illuminating the inside of the house with a cold white glow.

"Over there, on the table."

Ivan looked.

The table was actually a shelf that protruded from the wall beneath the window, attached by coarse wooden boards. It was littered with dust and bits of what looked like the remains of year-old meals—the kind one would rather not think about. To the side, a pile of dry chicken bones glowed ghostly white against the gray of old dust.

Something ball-shaped protruded from among the bones. It looked like no chicken skull Ivan had ever seen. In fact, it had eye and nose sockets, strangely similar to those Ivan had seen in an old graveyard. It was almost like—

He forced his eyes further along the shelf, to a beaten metal jug sitting next to a flat clay dish. The water in the jug glistened like a dark eye. It seemed to wink as it caught Ivan's gaze.

"Pour the water into the dish."

"What?" Ivan asked. "Why?"

"Are you daft, boy? Hurry. We don't have much time."

The jug was cool to the touch. Though dust thickly coated its dark metal sides, its suffused gleam made Ivan wonder what it was really made of. Back in the palace he'd once seen an old silver chalice, his father's most prized possession, that had had a similar glint hidden in the carvings of its exquisite workmanship. The jug he held now was not elaborately carved, but it looked, if anything, even more ancient in its frightful beauty than the one his father treasured.

The water did not splash as it hit the dusty clay surface. It filled the dish with the confidence of a body filling out the familiar shape of its favorite chair. The water *belonged* there. Yet, as it poured out of the jug, the jug itself did not become any emptier.

Ivan filled the dish to the brim and carefully put down the jug.

"Now look."

Wolf put his front paws on the table and together they bent over the still surface of the water.

At first all was dark. In the glinting moonlight Ivan even imagined he saw their reflections, barely distinguishable in the darkness. Then the splotches of moonlight became livelier, filling out the dull clay dish with their silvery glow. And then—

Ivan didn't catch the moment when the shapes reflected in the water came together into a picture. There was a field washed with the afternoon sun, and a great tree in the distance. The breeze rippled the tall grass, so that the field looked almost like a lake of gray-green water.

The picture moved. They followed the view over the grass to the side of the giant tree. Ivan could now see that the field ended in a jagged cliff just beyond. There was a stream of water, far below. And something white down there, something that oddly resembled the pile of chicken bones on the side of the table.

Ivan took a breath and stepped away from the dish. The vision faded.

"Now we know where your path lies," Wolf said slowly. "To the Cat. Oh, well."

He jumped down and made his way to the door. Behind him, steam rose off the surface of the clay dish, milky like the fog rising over the water in the early hour of the night. Then, the dish was dry again, covered with old dust as if nothing had touched it in ages.

Ivan found his voice. "What do you mean, the cat?"

Wolf gave him a long look.

Ivan followed the beast to the door. He knew when it was best not to wait for an answer.

In the dark entry area Wolf stopped so suddenly Ivan almost ran into him.

"What is it?" Ivan whispered.

Wolf turned, his muzzle pushing close to Ivan's ear, the beast's hot breath burning his cheek. "As we open the door and go outside, follow the path to the gate and on toward the forest. Don't step off the path, whatever you do. Don't run, whatever you think the danger is. And, most importantly, *don't look back.*"

They opened the door and slid out into the dusk. As they made their hasty way along the path, Ivan imagined he heard a creak behind him, as if someone opened the door and stood there, looking at their retreating shapes. It took all his strength not to turn, to continue walking, following Wolf's un-hurried trot along the path, out the gate, and further, over the nearest hill toward the distant shape of the looming forest.

As they reached the hedge, Ivan imagined he heard the distant thud of the door closing behind them. He realized he was trembling.

They walked for what seemed like hours before Wolf finally stopped.

"We camp here, boy," he said. "Make sure you rest well. You'll have much to do tomorrow."

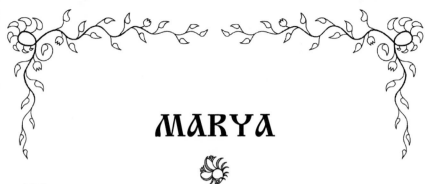

MARYA

The day I turned thirteen was the first day my Mirror told me I was the most beautiful woman in the world. Stunned, I stood and watched my reflection, a face that had never seemed to me to be particularly attractive. A pale narrow oval, for which my black hair, dark cherry lips, and green eyes seemed too richly colored. The most beautiful? Hmm...

Praskovia had come to dress me that day, her expression unusually solemn. She pulled out a black silk dress I had never worn before.

"Your father wants to see you, Marya."

I saw my father regularly in the great hall. During these audiences I walked to him across the flagstones, up to the chair carved from raven-black wood, and then he patted me on the head with a cool hand. There was nothing unusual in this request. Yet, I had felt a sting in Praskovia's words. Something had changed. But what?

I followed Praskovia down the winding staircase and through the narrow stone passages of the old castle. Her steady steps never slowed as we passed the turn that led down another flight of stairs to the great hall.

I wanted to ask a question but I kept my mouth shut. The Mistress of the Solstice never speaks in vain. I was taught well.

Was it today that I assumed my duties?

But then, what had happened to the previous Mistress? Had she given in to the power of Love?

The corridor widened as we walked down its last stretch to the heavy, metal-clad doors at the end. Praskovia raised her hand to knock, but the doors opened of their own accord. My father stood there.

He looked even more magnificent than I'd remembered.

He nodded to Praskovia, who bowed and glided away along the corridor. She never gave me as much as a glance.

"Come in, Marya," my father beckoned.

He waited for me to walk through the door and closed it behind me with a thud. I stood straight, trying to keep my eyes from darting about. It was the first time I'd been in my father's quarters, and despite a closely held fear, I was curious.

The furnishing of his chamber was as simple as mine. A stiff wooden bench, a desk with a large bottle of ink and a pile of parchment on one side. A shelf with thick, leather-clad volumes that bore the markings of centuries of heavy use. There was no bed. Then, I saw a door that led to the side, into what must have been an inner chamber. It took all I had to keep from stretching my neck to peek inside.

I started as I realized that my father was standing very close. I could sense his cool breath on my neck.

"I am told," my father said, "that you have grown to become the most beautiful woman in the world."

His hand swept aside a strand of my hair that had fallen against my cheek. The brush of his fingers, touching my skin, felt like a surge of power. I shivered.

"I believe," my father went on, "that it is time to teach you one of the most important lessons you must learn as the future Mistress of the Solstice."

His hand gently brushed my neck. I stood very straight, looking ahead, trying to fight off the shivers that engulfed my body.

"Today you will learn the difference between love and lust."

He stepped in front of me and cupped my face in his hands. They were cool and smooth, so soothing to the fire that slowly rose inside me.

"Remember, as the Mistress of the Solstice you must never love. It will try to find its way into your soul through the desires, the urges of your body to be with a man. You must learn to separate these feelings. Your body will try to trick you into believing there is only one man you want. That's how Love starts."

As he spoke, his hands were touching first my face, then my hair, my neck, my shoulders...He stepped closer and ran his deft fingers down my body, so that every cool touch through the thin silk of my new dress burned like fire. I shivered. I was powerless before this. I could no longer stand still. I moaned and sank into his arms.

"Can you feel it, Marya?" he whispered into my ear. "You want me, and no one else. You think all your happiness lies in my touch. You want for this never to stop."

"Yes, yes!" I whispered into his hair, pressing my cheek against his, clinging to him as if my life depended on it.

And then it was over. The enchantment was broken. He stepped away from me, leaving me helpless, shivering, aching for his touch. Lost.

I blinked.

"This is how it starts, Marya," he said. "You must learn to recognize it, and when you feel anything similar to what you feel now, here is what I want you to do."

He snapped his fingers and three men came through the door that led to the inner chamber. They were all dark, lean, and handsome, all wore open shirts that let me see their bare, hairless chests, the muscle playing under their skin. They looked young, only a few years older than me.

"These men," my father said, "will teach you to enjoy your body separately from your heart. They are skilled, and they will please you in many ways. They will stay with you until morning. Then, I will see you again."

"But, Father," I whispered, terrified.

"Are you defying me, Marya?"

I lowered my eyes. "No, Father."

"Good." He turned and walked out of the room.

The men were skilled indeed. And tireless, as they did everything in their power to make me enjoy my body. I wanted no part of it. Yet, as I had overcome my shame of the strange hands exploring places I thought only belonged to me, as my tears dried, I found a strange pleasure in what they did.

I never learned their names.

In the morning, my father blasted my three lovers to ashes in front of me. The youngest and gentlest of the three tried to escape, but there was no place to hide in the circular room with no furnishing but the low wooden bed, wide enough for five to sleep in.

I was afraid to raise my face. I didn't want Father to see my tears.

Mistress of the Solstice doesn't cry.

"Did you enjoy yourself?"

I nodded. I didn't want him to know the truth.

"Do you still long for me to touch you?" he asked.

I shuddered at the thought.

And then I understood. It had worked. I could never again think about love without remembering the horror, the humiliation of being handled by three men and then seeing them killed in front of my eyes.

The memory of their shameless hands as they tried to overcome my reluctance was etched right there, along with the memory of their screams as they squirmed on the floor, caught in the slow hellfire of my father's magic. It mixed with the memory of my father's cold hands on my neck, and his eyes, full of a dark glow that pierced me to my very soul.

If this was love, then I could never love again.

IVAN

"**I** still don't know why I bother with you, boy," Wolf said.

Ivan could see the grass of the fields through the hedge ahead, awash with the reddish light of the waning sun. He had to walk very fast to keep up. He took a breath to keep the panting out of his voice.

"What do you mean, a cat?"

"*The* cat," Wolf corrected him. "The cat all other cats come from. The Telltale Cat."

Ivan considered this.

"Cats don't tell tales," he ventured.

Wolf reached the opening between two birch trees and stopped on the edge of the field, just inside the forest hedge.

"Maybe stupid humans just don't listen."

Ivan took another deep breath. His legs hurt from the day-long march. His heart pounded.

"So, what am I facing?"

"Yourself," Wolf replied "And based on recent events, I must say you have no worse enemy."

Ivan shrugged. "It's no help being cryptic."

Wolf turned his muzzle toward Ivan. His yellow eyes beckoned. Ivan found himself sinking into the lupine gaze, drawn by the ancient, ruthless force it emanated.

There was no escape. He could no longer remember who he was. He knew nothing about his aim, his desire, his purpose. Nothing except the two yellow orbs that encompassed his whole being. His whole world.

And then it was gone. He was back at the hedge, the last sunbeams of the day caressing his skin. Birds chirped, and a mosquito next to his ear buzzed its bloodthirsty song.

Ivan. I am Ivan.

He shuddered.

Ivan the Fool.

"What you just felt was but a touch of the power that the Primals possess. Bayun the Cat's power is similar to mine. Similar, but different."

"How?" Ivan managed.

"Wolves live in packs. Their power is open to share with other beings. Cats are solitary. So, their power is not for sharing. Their power is aimed to take, not to give. *Never* to give."

"Why are we seeking his help, then? If he won't give us anything, what's the use?"

"*You* are seeking his help, because you got yourself into trouble even I can't save you from. And that, boy, is no small task. If Bayun refuses to help you, you're truly on your own."

"All right." Ivan sighed. "What should I do?"

"First, don't ask anything of him. If the beast senses you want something, you are lost."

"How am I going to learn things if I don't ask?"

"By listening. That's what I've been telling you all along. If you had just been *listening...*" Wolf growled and turned away.

Ivan waited.

"His tales always have a meaning, boy, and they're directed by the listener. You can figure things out if you just listen carefully. I know you can use your head. Sometimes."

"Anything else?"

"Yes. Remember who you are. Don't let him talk you into forgetting."

Ivan remembered the draw of Wolf's gaze. If the power of Bayun the Cat was similar, this advice would be hard to heed.

"Above all, don't confuse the real with the false."

"What?"

"The beast will try to confuse you, trick you with illusions, until you won't know what is true anymore. Don't let him. Think of anything you can that is real. Don't let go. Or else, you are lost."

For a second there was pity and sorrow in Wolf's gaze. Ivan looked away. This was much more unnerving than the contempt of last night.

"Good luck." Wolf turned to depart.

"Wait!" Ivan called out. "Are you just going to leave me like this?"

"Like what?"

Ivan shrugged. "I guess, I hoped you'd stay around... Until I'm—done."

Wolf rested his muzzle on Ivan's shoulder. "Remember, boy, cats and wolves don't 'stay around' each other. Ever. Not even in death."

He leapt past Ivan and disappeared behind a thick hazelnut bush. The fleshy leaves wavered, then went still in his wake.

The path was so thin that at times it was hard to find through the wavering grass. Obviously, Bayun's lair was not popular with visitors.

The mighty oak squatted on the hilltop like a monstrous bird on its perch, spreading wing-like branches over its wide nesting grounds. The earth rose under the pull of the massive roots, forming a hill as if by the sheer will of the ancient tree. It was hard to imagine that anything might have been there before the tree. Even the rocks, bared by the cliff behind it, looked small and uncertain by comparison, as if knobby root fingers had tucked them into place to finish off the impressive roost.

As Ivan made his way up the hill, he saw no movement. The path on the hill became more defined, curving around the tree like a loose rope thrown carelessly into the thick grass. It was barely visible in the long evening shadows.

Ivan paused, waiting.

"Anyone home?" he asked carefully.

There was a rustle in the branches above his head and, moments later, the ground on his left shook noiselessly. Even then, it appeared as if the large shape that blocked the waning sunlight had grown out of the grass, instead of dropping from the branches above. Its movements, though they looked slow and lazy in their quality, were so swift they were hard for the eye to follow.

Ivan stared.

It looked like a very large house cat, smaller than Wolf, yet too big to be confused with an ordinary animal. Sitting down, its head reached just above Ivan's waist. Its long fur was pitch-black, outlined against the blood-red sunset like a halo of darkness. Then Ivan saw the eyes.

The creature's eyes were jewel green and they shone out of the blackness, as if emanating a light of their own, bright even against the sunset background. Ivan shivered under their gaze as if he'd been burned with cold green hellfire.

It was the most beautiful creature Ivan had ever seen.

The giant cat stirred.

"Ivan the Fool of the Twelfth Kingdom," he mused. His voice was soft and deep, like a purr. He seemed to whisper, yet the sound echoed through Ivan like thunder.

A cat's face filled Ivan's vision and he saw, for a brief moment, a pink tongue flick out of its mouth lo lick razor-sharp fangs. Then it was gone.

"What do you seek, boy?" Bayun whispered. "What tale do you want to hear? Perhaps, of your own deeds turned into a song? Listen..."

The soft purr of his voice filled Ivan's ears. The cat's voice drew, no less captivating, than the green of his gaze. Instead of words, images filled Ivan's head, as if he was watching events take place in front of his eyes. No, not watching— acting. Living them through the soft purr of the cat's tale.

The evening smell of damp grass filled Ivan's nostrils. He was no longer on the hilltop under the giant oak. He was facing the oak, but *the oak was gnarled, looming over the straight path that led to the castle wall.*

At first glance it seemed safe. One could walk right through without stopping.

But there was a web of water droplets crossing the path. The deadly trap on the way to the Mistress's tower. If one walked through, one would be lost. Ivan would lose his mind and never reach the castle. He would walk out into the swamp and perish in its bottomless depths...

This was not how it happened in real life, but more beautiful, like in a song. Any discrepancies did hot matter as he immersed himself in the tapestry of the cat's tale.

MARYA

Ivan in the Mirror reached out and touched a hanging droplet of water. His hand followed in a spiral pattern, and with a sigh the magical mist unraveled itself, disappearing like thin smoke into the night wind.

I drew away from the Mirror.

How had this boy learned to unravel my mist? It had taken my father and I a month to put it in place. No one was supposed to know how to remove it.

Perhaps I'd do better to learn his story from the start.

"Tell me about his past," I ordered the Mirror.

The fog disappeared to reveal a frightened little boy perched on a thin branch of an apple tree. The boy's face was lean and freckled, but I could easily recognize his eyes, blue like cornflowers.

Two older boys stood on the ground laughing, swinging the tree back and forth.

"Hurry up, Ivan!" the oldest boy shouted. "Get that apple over there!"

"Will it really give our father his youth back, Vassily?" the other boy on the ground whispered doubtfully.

"Of course not, Fedor, you idiot!" Vassily hissed back, shaking the tree violently.

"I can't get the apple, brothers!" Ivan shouted from above. "The tree is trying to throw me off!"

"That's because it doesn't want you to get the apple! Do you think our father's youth is easy to get?" Vassily answered, smothering an evil laugh.

"All right!" Ivan shouted, and in the Mirror I saw a tear run down his pale strained face.

106

I watched the pictures flash by, so absorbed I forgot to tell my Mirror to stop or to condense the sad tale.

I saw little Ivan fall from the tree just as he grabbed for the apple hanging from the furthest branch.

I saw his brothers watch him crawl on the ground—Vassily with cold satisfaction, Fedor with mild concern—as young Ivan fought tears of pain, smearing the blood dripping from his nose all over his face with the back of his hand.

I saw them present the case to their father, the Tzar, in a way that made little Tzarevich Ivan look like a complete idiot who'd suddenly imagined that an ordinary apple from their orchard could make their father young again.

And I watched such stories go on and on until, against Ivan's protests, he firmly and finally became known to everyone in his household as Ivan, the Fool.

I admired the evil wit of Tzarevich Vassily who set his traps, one by one, with the skill of a born schemer. It was obvious to anyone, that of the three sons of the widowed Tzar it was not the wicked Vassily, or the simple-minded Fedor, but Ivan with his sunny personality for whom his father had the highest hopes. And so his older brother cleverly made sure that his father's hopes were diverted from Ivan to himself.

He played on Ivan's good nature and love for his father to make the boy do the stupidest things. Their six years' difference in age made Vassily sound so mature and honest, both to little Ivan and to their elderly father.

Vassily's superb mind invented more and more complicated yet seemingly logical tasks for his little brother, which, combined with Ivan's desire to help, infallibly proved him to be a fool in the end. It took a fool indeed to believe Vassily after so many failures. And yet, every time I heard Vassily speak in the Mirror, I felt I could believe him myself.

Ivan, at Vassily's bidding, went out into the middle of the town plaza to kneel, sprinkling the road dust onto his head. Vassily had told his youngest brother that the Crossroads man—his own invention fashioned after Leshy and his kind—

would then come and grant Ivan three wishes. As Ivan was brought before his father, dirt-covered and defiant, I saw him give Vassily a long look. He was getting older and wiser. But the damage had been done.

"Enough," I told the Mirror, taking a deep breath and shaking off the misery I'd just witnessed. I'd made the mistake of letting my compassion slip my guard. There was nothing terrible in what I'd seen. It wasn't an unusual game, and the best man always won.

"Show me why Ivan came to our kingdom," I ordered.

Again I saw the same palace in the Twelfth Kingdom, but this time the Ivan I saw was much older, a young man, not yet in his full strength, but already so painfully similar to the image in my head.

What is it that gives him such power? He is a simple-minded fool, kind, trusting, and good-natured. Everything I was taught to despise in a man.

Vassily was right. Yet I couldn't stop watching.

Ivan's father spoke in a voice full of concern. "It is a hard time for our kingdom, my son. The evil Tzar Kashchey of the Thirty Ninth kingdom demands that we pay tribute. He has destroyed many lands that lie to the east. I have no choice. Yet, if I accede to his demands, it would weaken us so that we would not be able to defend ourselves. At such a time, perhaps it would be better if you stayed?"

Kashchey, I thought. My father's hand reached far indeed. I felt a surge of pride for the power of our kingdom. Blessed be Kupalo and His ancient powers.

"I must go, Father," Ivan said gently. "I am not of much help to you here. Yet, I may come across something useful in the other kingdoms. Besides—"

The old man nodded.

"It is a tradition, I know," he said. "We send young men out into the world before they come of age. Your brother, Vassily, rode out six years ago and returned last year with beautiful Tzarevna Varvara from the Third kingdom, a Tzar's daughter he rescued from the evil Tzar Kashchey."

What a lie! I thought. Nobody had ever rescued a maiden from my father. Vassily had turned whatever happened to his credit again.

"I am proud of Vassily. He came back a hero, with a beautiful bride, and I hope he will succeed me to make a great ruler for our kingdom."

I, for one, agreed with the old Tzar's choice of heir. Vassily, smart and ruthless, would make a good ruler. Not a do-gooder like Ivan.

"Now, Fedor, he came back empty-handed. He didn't gain much glory, but he had a chance to see the world and to gain some skills on his own. You, Ivan," the old man hesitated, looking at his youngest son with discomfort. "Must you really go?"

I realized I was clenching my teeth. What would I ever do if my own father showed such distrust in me? I think such a look alone could kill me. But the Ivan in the Mirror didn't seem to care. Or was he so skillful at hiding his pain?

"Yes, I must go, father," he answered with his usual easy smile. "I don't want to be your shame for the rest of your life."

His smile was overwhelming. It glowed like a stream of light, it absorbed his father's protests, as steady and inevitable as time itself.

"Gods be with you, Tzarevich Ivan," the old man said, blessing him with a weary hand. "Right or wrong, you are my son and I love you."

The old man turned and re-entered the palace, his head bent, and Ivan rode away.

He needs a better horse, I thought as I watched the skinny disaster of an animal putting one unsteady foot in front of another on the dusty road. Why, this beast must be at least twenty years old, if not more. Hardly a befitting steed for a young Tzarling.

I ordered the Mirror to stop.

I could spare no more time for this. I needed to settle the question of who had betrayed the secret of my father's Death, and how to get the Needle back before it landed in unfriendly hands through its bearer's foolishness.

The Raven wasn't on his perch. In fact, he'd been missing since my last nocturnal adventure.

"Show me Raven!" I told my Mirror.

IVAN

Ivan stirred.

For the life of him, he couldn't remember who he was or why he was sitting on the grass beneath a tall oak, listening—

—to the cat's purring tales...

The soft, whisper-like voice drew him in. He couldn't hear the words. Only images that poured into his head with an intensity so overwhelming for his tired mind—

—so hard...

A woman, ancient as the trees, stretched her gnarled arms over the still body of a warrior. His severed head lay next to the bloodied stump of the neck, its eyes still open. Under the mask of death the face was very young, boyish.

The woman chanted, passing her hands, dark and roughened as if covered with tree bark, over the still, outstretched limbs. Then she dropped her arms to her sides and sat still.

—purr, purr...

A furry shape leaned against him. He reached out and absentmindedly scratched its ear—

—The old woman labored to her feet, put two fingers into her mouth, and whistled. The sound was so strong that the wind it raised flattened the leaves of the nearby trees. A thunder rolled through their branches in response, and a large, heavy object landed next to her, planting itself deep into the damp forest floor.

It was a giant mortar, but instead of a pestle, a broom stuck its bristled head out of the mortar's opening.

The woman bent down and lifted the dead body with the care of a mother lifting her child out of a crib. One marveled at such strength in a woman so old. Yet, in the tale, it all made sense.

She carefully wrapped the severed head in a cloth and put it into

111

her apron pocket. Then she eased the body into the mortar and jumped in herself.

A broom appeared in her hand. Leaning out of the mortar, she swept the forest floor. The swirl of wind in its wake lifted the mortar and its load into the air, raised it higher and higher, and carried it above the trees and into the distance.

—purr—purr—

He was so thirsty. If only he could have but a drop of water.

He lifted his tired head, but there was no water in sight. And the tale drew him, caressed him as it flowed on the waves of the cat's deep purr...

It was another place, many kingdoms away. The old woman had climbed out of the mortar and was searching for something. A bloodied lock of blond hair stuck out of her bulging apron pocket.

Why do we keep coming back to this tale? The man is already dead, isn't he?

He wanted to weep for the fallen warrior, but he had no tears left.

No water.

The woman settled into the thick grass, humming softly to herself. It was a tune both familiar and strange. One could swear it was the most common song, yet as soon as the sounds died out, he couldn't remember any of them.

I—remember—nothing...

The woman stirred, suddenly alert. The tinkling sound of water disturbed the forest stillness. It was soft and pleasant, just like the woman's song.

She kept singing as she crept through the grass toward the sound of the water. And there, at the side of the small hilltop, was a stream.

The woman took out the severed head and laid it on the grass. From the same pocket she produced a vial and filled it from the stream. She moved carefully, as if afraid to touch the water. Then she gave a shrill whistle and the heavy mortar came stumbling toward her through the forest undergrowth. The headless body dangled over its edge, arms flapping against the side.

The old woman took the body out and spread it on the ground.

She took great care to adjust the head to the body, pressing it against the stump of the neck so that the young man looked merely wounded. With one hand, she held the head tightly against the neck. With the other, she sprinkled the water from the vial onto the wound.

The liquid foamed as it touched the skin. The foam consumed the blood and covered the cut. It bubbled, pristine white on the creamy white skin. And then—

. . . purr, purr. . .

The cut was no longer there. The head was melded on its neck just like it was supposed to. There was no sign that only moments ago the head and the body were separate from one another.

The woman kissed the vial and sprinkled again, this time on the corpse's forehead. There was a sigh as it touched the skin. And a change. At first Ivan couldn't name it. The body was still pale, but it was no longer—

—no longer dead.

The fallen warrior stirred. His eyelids fluttered open and he looked up at her. And now tears stood in the woman's eyes. They brimmed her wrinkled eyelids and ran down her face, making their way among the folds of her wrinkled skin, dry like ancient bark.

She cried for the living where she had no tears for the dead.

"Have I—fallen asleep?" the man asked. Through the hoarseness of the freshly mended throat his voice was as young as his appearance. No more than a boy.

"You slept too long, Ilia." The woman nodded, smiling through her tears. "Time to wake up."

A cat's face filled Ivan's vision. The jewel-green eyes were no longer dreamy.

"I am tired of you, boy," the cat said. "I think you are ready to jump off the cliff."

Ivan didn't question it. He clambered to his feet, stiff from too many hours of sitting on the hard ground, and wordlessly walked toward the precipice beyond.

He looked over the edge. There were bones down there. Many bones. He could just make out the white balls of skulls scattered among them, far below.

A pack of crows on the nearby boulders looked at him expectantly.

"Go on, boy," the cat said from behind. "Jump."

He took another step forward.

Why did I come here?

Who am I?

He was thirsty, so thirsty he couldn't think straight.

Water.

Am I here because of the water?

He turned and looked at the cat.

"Water," he croaked with a dry mouth. The sound of his voice was so strange, so ugly compared to the cat's deep purr.

"There's water down below," the cat told him. "After you jump, you can have all you want."

It made sense.

He turned back to the cliff.

But why had he come here in the first place? If only he could remember what had possessed him to look for water up here, on the hilltop, when there was so much water down below.

Was there something else he needed?

He thought of the old woman from the tale. She'd used water to bring a man back to life. At least he could remember that much. He couldn't escape the thought that there was something important in that tale. Something he was missing.

He couldn't jump off the cliff...yet.

"You're wasting time, boy," the cat said irritably. "One more step."

Ivan reached inside his shirt, searching. There was something he had to remember.

His searching fingers came across something tucked deep into the shirt, and emerged holding a flower. A crumpled plant, withered almost beyond recognition. Two flowers on one stem, purple and yellow.

He held it out to the cat.

"Ivan-and-Marya?" the cat asked. "Why are you giving me that?"

Ivan-and-Marya.

114

Ivan—
—and Marya.
And then he remembered.

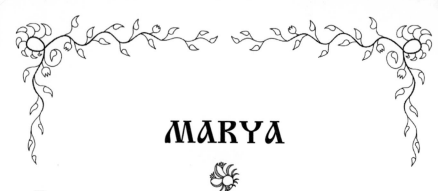

MARYA

It was pitch-dark in the woods. The night air enfolded me in cold waves, carrying the fresh smell of wet earth and the distant wails of a night bird. In my dove shape I was not fit to fly in the dark. I narrowly avoided being skewered on several wickedly protruding branches and was beginning to think of turning back into my human form when Raven called out for me.

"Stay on that branch, Marya. I am flying over."

Wind ruffled my feathers as he settled beside me, digging his claws into the smooth, paper-white bark of the birch branch.

I hoped he'd say something, but he just sat there in silence.

"So," I began after a long pause. "I thought you were friends with my father. How could you tell this boy, this fool, about my father's death?"

To my surprise I sensed a smile in his voice as he replied: "There are things you don't understand, Marya."

"Then maybe you could try and explain it to me." Why did I feel wrong? What had disturbed me so deeply? As if it were I who had to answer for my deeds to Raven, and not the other way around.

Raven didn't reply immediately, but when he did, his voice didn't waver. "He is not an ordinary boy, Marya. And he is certainly not a fool. You felt that too."

"You know not to talk about my feelings, Raven. I have none."

"You are in worse danger than you realize, Marya. And that puts all of us into danger as well."

Now I caught it. He wasn't smiling at all. The thing I

sensed in his voice was the strain of keeping his voice level. But I was too angry to care.

"I suppose this is why you helped the boy along?" I snapped.

"I had no choice, Marya. He captured me and forced me bargain for my life."

I stared. Raven was an Immortal, nearly invincible. *No one* could capture Raven, or force him to do anything.

"He *captured* you?"

Raven's expression was unreadable. "I told you, he is not an ordinary boy, Marya. He had me in his power."

I opened my mouth, but no sound came. Dove throat was much too weak to express the entire richness of human emotions.

"How did he do it?" I finally managed.

"He had the Net."

"You don't mean—the *Net*?" My voice faltered again.

Raven only shrugged.

I still couldn't believe it. This *boy*? How could he possibly get Raven's Bane? How could he possibly know about its existence and whereabouts when even I, Raven's closest companion, had no idea about it? A chill ran down my spine that had nothing to do with the cool night air.

I felt the need to speak to talk it through with Raven, as if talking could help. "How could he possibly find it? Who could have told him?"

Raven shrugged again. "Only the Immortals know about my Bane. I had entrusted it to *Leshy*, the trickiest of them all. He swore an unbreakable oath to keep it safe. It is the only thing in the world that is able to render me helpless."

I opened and closed my beak, struggling to find my voice. *Leshy.* "How could the old Forest Man give it up?" I shivered. *No one* could hoax things from the old creature. Not even my father.

Raven cocked his head and looked at me sideways. "There is the riddle game."

I scoffed, an uncomfortable sound through a bird's throat.

"You cannot seriously think the boy challenged Leshy and won the riddle game. I've talked to him. He seemed... simpleminded. Daft." And so warm, vigorous, kind... The memory of the tenderness in his eyes, the warmth of his hand on mine, made me ache.

"I talked to him too, Marya. And yes, he could be all these things, but there's something in him that escapes common logic. Such—"

"—innocence," I said.

"—willpower."

We stopped and looked at each other.

I had never remembered before feeling so vulnerable. Frightened. What doom were we headed to?

Raven's voice sank to a half-whisper. "When he captured me, he knew exactly what to ask me for. Believe me, I didn't make it easy for him to learn the truth. And yet, he got exactly what he came for. And used it."

"How?" I insisted. "How did he know he must question you, and no one else? It would have been so much easier for him to approach, say, Praskovia."

"If he did, he would be dead by now."

"Yes." I shivered at the thought. Praskovia. Her motherly looks were often deceiving, I knew that of her. She had always been kind to me, but deep inside she could be sterner than my father.

Raven shuffled on the branch, turning to face me. "None of us can imagine how much the boy must have gone through to catch me. He knew who I was. He knew I was the one he needed, at any cost. Granted, he was a bit rusty on the questioning bit, but in the end he figured out what questions to ask to get what he wants. Do you understand, Marya?"

I didn't understand. *I* was daft, *I* was the fool. "So, what does he want now?"

"Didn't he tell you?"

"He asked for my hand."

Raven's eyes widened in astonishment. "He did?"

"Yes."

"What a fool!"

"Yes. Just like his nickname."

Raven shook his head. "Nicknames are such a burden at times."

"Why, Raven? Why would he escape so many traps, do so many impossible things only to put himself in my power?"

"Perhaps his downfall was your beauty?"

I shrugged. "Perhaps." I didn't believe it any more than Raven did. I wasn't even sure who was in whose power. There was a bond between me and this boy, linking us like the flower he had tried to offer me back in my tower. *Ivan-and-Marya*.

I longed to change back into human shape. I longed to get away, to the safety of my chamber, and to hide my face in Praskovia's large bosom as I used to do in days gone forever.

I didn't want to face this.

"I didn't tell the boy about the Needle, Marya. I would have, if he'd asked me, because I was bound by the Net. But he didn't ask. He already knew where it was."

I became aware of the silence, disturbed only by the distant noises of the night forest. I stirred, trying to silence the maddening questions endlessly circling in my head.

Who *was* this boy?

How could he know so much?

Who was helping him?

And, why?

"All he wanted to know was how to get into your tower without running into your traps. I told him everything, Marya. I had no choice."

"My father mentioned a prophecy."

"Oh, yes. The prophecy." Again I heard a smile in his voice, and wondered what true emotion it hid.

"I didn't know there was one. I was taught by you and my father not to believe in them."

Raven chuckled. "A wise teaching. Prophecies are nonsense; no more than rhymes that people make up to amuse themselves. It is the words that make prophecies that are to

119

be feared."

"How so?"

"People are foolish. They believe in words. They repeat those silly rhymes, carry them from village to village, until everyone recites them with reverence and stores them away at the backs of their minds. And then the evil comes. Those hungry for power find out prophecies and make them come true. It does not take much for common villagers to believe."

"But how could one make a rhyme come true?"

"Say, there is a rhyme that tells of a true king who would come dressed as a beggar in the dead of winter, produce the Sword of Doom and cut down the old tree by the well to open the way for a new spring."

"And?"

"And then, somebody decides to win this kingdom over. All they have to do is find a handsome woodcutter, dress him in rags, give him a sword strong enough to chop wood, and— there you have it. All he has to do is show up. The people will do the rest for him. They *want to* believe."

"There is still the matter of a new spring."

"You'd be amazed what people would be willing to believe for a true king."

"So, what does our prophecy say?"

The Raven recited, in a deep solemn voice:

> *"The power of Kupalo goeth forth into ages,*
> *Yet rule of immortal doth carry its doom.*
> *On the night of the Solstice, a hero of legend,*
> *Cometh marked by an arrow through turmoil and gloom.*
>
> *His guides are the creatures of magic and wisdom,*
> *His strength is no weapon, but fire in his eyes.*
> *He carrieth death for the rule of the kingdom,*
> *He bringeth new life for the new sacrifice."*

I considered it. It didn't make sense.

"That's all?" I asked in disbelief. "How do you know what

it means?"

"It's a prophecy, Marya, a rhyme. It doesn't mean anything. Yet, it can be interpreted in many ways. Since your father insists on calling himself Immortal, and there are many who want to see the end to his rule, we all have been on the lookout for the appropriate signs."

"Such as—?"

"Such as a boy with unexpected powers, who happens to wonder into our kingdom almost on the eve of the Solstice. Such as—certain signs that make everyone wonder who this boy really is."

"You can hardly call this one a hero of legend."

"He doesn't have to be. It's about the signs."

"Signs?"

The Raven sighed and ruffled his feathers, settling up on the branch. "You need to give me and your father a bit more time to sort this out, Marya. Trust us."

"I do," I said. "But maybe you should also trust me? The boy has already once caught me unawares. It would have helped if I'd been prepared."

Raven only shook his head.

"How do you know there's a connection between the rhyme and the boy?" I insisted. "How do you know a prophecy is even involved? What makes you think this boy is different from any other fool who comes to seek my hand?"

"This rhyme," Raven ruffled his feathers again, "is almost as old as the Solstice itself. Of course, we don't know for sure, but we aren't the only ones taking it seriously. There are many who would like to see this one come true."

"How do you know he is the one to fear?"

"He has a birthmark on his shoulder. It looks exactly like an arrow."

"An arrow-shaped birthmark?" I scoffed. "I stopped believing such tales when I was five. It must be a trick. Nothing that soap and water couldn't take care of. Come, Raven. Such a possibility surely must have crossed your mind?"

"Of course it did, Marya. You are missing the point. It

Anna Kashina

is not about the boy. It is about those who are behind him, helping him to bring down your father's rule. And, whether it is magic or cunning, we have to deal with it."

"How?"

"By learning what it is we are dealing with. Who is our enemy?"

"A boy. Perhaps a talented one, but no hero for certain. Why do you think there is more to it?"

"Perhaps no more than a boy," Raven said quietly. "But there are things about him. Have you noticed his eyes, Marya?"

His eyes. Cornflowers on a bright sunny day. The mere thought made me warm.

"It couldn't have been easy to find a boy who fits the rhyme so well. Think about it."

I did. The rhyme did fit. And yet, when someone talked about fire in the eyes that can serve as a weapon, they usually meant something else—like the cold hellfire of my father's eyes that could destroy his enemies with a single glance. Not the warm, mischievous fire that invited a smile. And a longing. Oh, such longing...

I grasped on to the shreds of my sanity. "But a prophecy has to fit exactly, doesn't it? Not just sort of. And, according to the rhyme, he's supposed to come on the night of the Solstice. It seems that your magic hero is a little early."

The Raven gave me a thoughtful look.

"What was the task you gave him, Marya?"

"To find the Hidden Stream and bring back the Water of Life by the Solstice."

"That gives him almost a fortnight. What makes you think he won't do it?"

"Here are my reasons, if you will." I forced myself to speak evenly, as if answering not a mockery but a real question. "It takes at least six months to walk from here to the Hidden Stream and back, perhaps three on horseback, if he has a really good horse. Besides, the stream is called 'hidden' for a reason. It will only reveal itself to an Immortal if he knows the

122

right song. Yet, an Immortal cannot touch its waters. Why, in the past thousand years only Baba Yaga has used the water, once, to bring back a dead warrior she fancied. As far as I know, she used all of the water she had, and no one, mortal or immortal, could ever convince her to go back and find the stream again. So, our magical hero will either come back too late, or empty-handed, in both of which cases he will be killed. If of course he comes back at all."

"Perhaps your task has given us the advantage we need," he agreed. "It was a stupid move, to ask for your hand. Of course, he is not on foot. And his mount is not a horse."

"Of course not. It has to be no less than a creature of magic and wisdom, to fit into your rhyme. But who could it be? Zmei Gorynich the Fire Serpent, perhaps? Or has Solovei-Razboinik, the Mugger Nightingale, decided to serve him out of the goodness of his heart?"

"Why don't you go home and ask your Mirror?" Raven stretched his wings.

I felt very tired. I didn't want to think of the boy anymore, of his eyes, of his birthmark—whatever shape it was—or his magic steed. I'd given him a good task and he was going to die. And I, Mistress of the Solstice, had other things to do, not the least of which was to get out of this forest without skewering myself on a branch my dove eyes could not see.

"I will go back," I said. "I may even talk to my Mirror, if I have time. But I think you worry too much."

"Perhaps," Raven said. "Perhaps."

I flapped my dove wings and rose into the air, starting my slow journey through the thicket of branches. Back to my stone tower in the Tzar's castle.

IVAN

Wolf was waiting at the forest hedge. He had a full bucket of water standing next to him.

Ivan stumbled to the bucket, dropped on all fours, and drank as much as he could. When he felt his stomach fill up like a grain sack at full harvest, he pulled back with regret that he could drink no more, and sank down heavily next to Wolf.

"Well?" Wolf asked.

Ivan exhaled, catching his breath, forcing his tongue to move inside his mouth. It still felt dry, as if he hadn't gulped half a bucket of water just now. "Baba Yaga. She is the one who can make it there fast enough. She also knows the song that can make the stream reveal itself. And maybe she still has half a vial of water stowed away somewhere."

Wolf stiffened. Ivan noticed but was too weak to care why. "And I assume you, boy, believe that she would be kind enough to give it to you."

Ivan didn't respond. It was nice to have Wolf his old self again. It was even nicer to be alive. He didn't feel like arguing.

Wolf sighed. "It's been three days. I would never have thought you could last that long."

"Neither would I," Ivan admitted. "But thanks, anyway."

He lifted the bucket to his lips again, feeling the water splash around in his stomach. But he was still thirsty. He felt as if he would be thirsty for the rest of his life.

"Don't drink it all at once. You'll burst."

Ivan put the bucket down regretfully.

"I suggest you wash yourself with whatever's left," Wolf said, "and then we get up and go. We have very little time."

It was impossible to see any distance in the eerie gloom of the dense forest undergrowth. Walking became more and more difficult. Sticky branches grasped clothes and fur, as if trying to prevent the intruders from going any further. Every step through the moss-covered mud was a struggle.

"Are you sure she lives out here?"

There was a growl and a muffled curse before the answer came.

"It clears up over there." Wolf sounded as if his mouth were full of leaves. Ivan thought best not to ask.

The ground began to rise. Ivan's feet no longer produced the smacking sound they'd made as he'd dragged them through the mud. The undergrowth of aspen, raspberry, and sickly fir gave way to the healthier thickness of young birch and hazel. The eerie forest dimness acquired some shades of yellow, reminding Ivan that somewhere out there the world was bathed in the afternoon sunlight.

He spotted the purple and yellow of Ivan-and-Marya and bent to pick a flower. After his encounter with Bayun the Cat, he'd promised himself he would always carry one around.

Only when he straightened again did he become aware of the clearing that seemed to have crept up and opened itself right in front of him. How could he forget that Ivan-and-Marya always grew near the edge of the trees?

A strange object dominated the center of the clearing, imposing, like a noble boyar in a village marketplace. It was technically a house, an *izba* built of unevenly hewn logs. The beams of its thatched roof were carved in ornate images of a raven and a wolf, so masterfully that their fur and feathers seemed real, their deeply set eyes watching the intruders. The house also had a small and rather murky window that looked badly in need of a wash. What lay below, however, didn't make any sense.

The *izba* was standing on a pair of thick poles, ending in tripods at the bottom that made them look more than anything like giant bird legs. As Ivan watched in fascination, the legs stepped from place to place, making the whole contraption look like a giant square chicken pecking in a yard.

A chicken wearing a house on its body.

"One thing," Wolf whispered into Ivan's ear. "You'll have to do all the talking."

"Why?"

Wolf looked away. For a moment he almost seemed embarrassed.

"Because I said so," he snarled. "This is your mess we're fixing, remember?"

Ivan shrugged and focused on the chicken-legged house. It wandered a short distance toward them and stopped, as if noticing the intruders for the first time. The murky window watched them like a wary eye.

Ivan stepped forward.

"Um," he began. "Would you be so kind as to, um, turn your door to me, little house?"

The contraption appeared to hesitate. Then, slowly, it turned around, revealing a coarse wooden door, swinging open. In fact, Ivan noticed, it had a broken hinge.

He carefully approached the gaping doorway.

"Anyone home?" he called out.

A rustle echoed in the gloom inside. Then a voice said:

"Do I smell fresh meat? Has young human flesh brought itself to the old woman's door?"

Ivan hesitated. The voice didn't sound old at all. It could have belonged to a healthy matron, one of those responsible for all the opinions formed at the village well. Yet, Bayun's tale depicted Baba Yaga as an old hag. An ancient woman, old as the trees.

How should he address her? If she was indeed ancient, he should respectfully call her "grandmother". And yet, if she was young, he should call her "mother", or even "sister". If he did it wrong, the whole visit might prove useless.

Ivan took a breath.

"Can I come in, old mother?" he called out.

There was a pause. Then, more rustling and a chuckle.

"Fresh meat that insults a woman he cannot even see by calling her old," she said. "Well, I don't mind. Rude boys taste the same as polite ones. At least, he found his own way to my kettle. Fine by me. Mayhap you would be good enough to bring along some wood to feed the fire?"

Ivan stepped forward and peered inside. It was a small and very dirty room. The entire left wall was occupied by a stove of the usual village type. Its flat top, *lezhanka*, the warmest place in the house, served as a bed, wide enough for two people to lie on.

An old woman, ancient as the trees, stretched on top of the *lezhanka*, her skin dark and wrinkled like tree bark. Her hair was disheveled, her face stained with soot, but her eyes gleamed brightly as she surveyed the visitor.

It was obvious from her looks that he had chosen the right address, not making her seem ancient by calling her "grandmother" and yet respecting her age by adding "old".

"A pretty one," she said. "Come closer, boy, I want to feel how tender you are. My teeth aren't what they used to be, you know. The last lad that ended up here was much too bony for this old hag."

She brought out a hand from under the blanket and Ivan saw a large bone clenched in the gnarled fingers. He couldn't tell for sure, but by the size of it, the bone could well be human.

Ivan shivered. "Why would you want to eat me, old mother?"

"Why not?" she asked with what seemed like genuine interest.

"Because—" He struggled for the right words. Put like this, the question did make sense. "I may be more useful alive."

"Useful?" She chuckled again. "For what?"

Ivan threw another glance around the room. The floor was barely visible under a thick layer of dust and dirt that rolled on the floor as the hut stepped from leg to leg, probably tired of standing still. The window was so soiled it barely let through any light. The kettle on the stove was covered with so much soot and grease it seemed shapeless. The smells of dirt, old age, and stagnation hung in the room. It wasn't over-whelming, but after the freshness of the forest outside, it was too much to ignore.

"I could help you tidy up your house. It seems like no one has done it for a while. I could also fix your door. And maybe put new grass into your mattress. It looks like it might need some."

"A sweet-spoken one." She appeared to consider his offer. "Very nice of you, boy, but you said nothing of cooking me any food. And if I starve, I'll have no use for a tidy house, eh?"

"I could catch you some wild rabbits," Ivan suggested.

"Rabbits." She smacked her lips. "They're not as good as human flesh, you know. Not sweet enough. Yet, they're ten-der, and if you add beetroot to the stew, it might just make it sweet enough for the old woman's teeth. But—" she shook her head, "—you're just like all the other silly boys. Trying to out-smart the old woman. You think I'll let you go rabbit-huntin' and you'll run away. No, boy, the kettle it is for you!"

"I'll stay," Ivan promised. "I won't go anywhere. My friend will catch the rabbits for you while I clean up. How many would you like?"

"Your friend?" She clambered off the stove bed to peer out the door, and for the first time Ivan had a good look at her eyes. They were yellow, with vertical pupils. Just like a wolf's.

"Where?" she asked.

Ivan turned. Wolf was nowhere to be seen.

MARYA

The girl's dark blond hair, loose from its braid, reached down almost to her knees. I hadn't been mistaken. It was thick enough to look pleasing when let loose. Very few girls had hair strong enough to grow to that length.

Her face was still swollen with tears and her pale-blue eyes studied me shyly and with fear.

"What is your name?" I asked as she walked for me to the center of the room. She moved in a smooth, sliding gait that made her appear as if she glided above the floor, her head and shoulders floating straight, never bouncing with a step. Village girls acquired this walk carrying a *koromyslo* on their shoulders, a long board with a bucket of water attached to each end, the most efficient device to fetch water from the well. During a sometimes long walk, smooth, gliding steps made water splash much less. And mastering this skill certainly made some peasant women look more elegant and majestic than noble ladies.

"I am Alyona, mistress," the girl answered in a half-whisper.

She was afraid of me, no doubt, and of what awaited her on the Solstice night. I had to make sure she was suitable in every way.

"How old are you, Alyona?" I asked, making my voice soft and gentle.

"I will be seventeen next week, mistress. I mean... I am sixteen." Two large tears rolled down her cheeks.

I took the girl by the hands, sending some calm into her, making her shivers quiet down, just as my father had taught me to do. Who else but my father would know how to quieten a frightened girl with magic?

"You understand, Alyona, that it is a great honor to be chosen for the Solstice. You will be sacrificed for the good of our land. You will help all the villages in the kingdom survive another season. Only the most beautiful and worthy maidens receive this honor."

"I am very honored, mistress." Another, smaller tear ran down her face.

I tried to ignore her tears, looking instead at her lowered eyelashes, the soft curve of her profile, the slender neck. The rest was concealed by the baggy dress she was still wearing, but my serving women assured me her body looked good all the way down. *Sadness becomes her,* I thought. *Her looks will do.*

"Are you a virgin, Alyona?" I asked.

She blushed so deeply that even her neck turned crimson, and she gave a slight nod of her head.

I knew she was, but I wanted her to say it.

"Are you?" I pressed. "Answer me!"

"I am, mistress, I swear I am!" Another tear slipped down her cheek.

"Good." I smiled at her. "I think you will be perfect for your important role. You won't betray our trust, will you, Alyona?"

"I will not, mistress," she said firmly, biting her pretty lower lip.

That was the secret of dealing with peasants. Say the right words and they will serve you for the rest of their lives. However long that might be.

"From now on, you are named the Chosen One, the Sacred Maiden of the Summer Solstice. May you serve our land well."

I stepped forward, placed my hands on her cheeks, and kissed her on the forehead. My kiss was the official seal on this pact of death. It left a star-shaped mark on her forehead, visible only on the night of the Solstice.

"My servants will see to your needs and help you get ready," I said and waved to my maids to lead her away.

As I approached my father's quarters, I heard muffled screams coming from the inner room. I hesitated. I didn't like to disturb my father when he was with one of his women. Especially not when he was in a mood to be rough, but time was precious and there were questions I needed to ask him.

I pushed open the heavy door and the hinges squealed. My father liked to be warned of visitors. I was glad, as it meant I was spared from catching him unawares.

A woman's garments were scattered on the floor of the main room, a boyar's daughter by the look of it, though it was really none of my business. My father was free to have his fun whichever way he liked. If these girls were foolish enough to get caught with him, it was their problem.

There was a smirk on his face when he came out of his inner chamber to meet me.

"I need to talk to you, Father."

He smiled, but kept his silence. He knew why I'd come, of course, but he wouldn't make it easy for me.

I held his gaze. "I talked to Raven before dawn."

"And?"

"He told me the prophecy."

"So?"

"Why didn't you tell me, Father? Why did you let me face the boy unprepared?"

"I thought you didn't believe in prophecies," he said with dry amusement.

"I thought you were the one who taught me not to," I parried.

We studied one another for a moment.

"The Raven suggested that I ask the Mirror why the boy came to our kingdom. And who is helping him."

"A wise precaution."

"Will you come and see it with me?" And with a glance toward the inner chamber, I added, "When you can."

He shrugged. "Let's go. We can't afford to waste time."

Anna Kashina

He turned and walked out of the room and I followed, forcing thoughts of what we left in my father's inner chamber out of my head. It was none of my business.

Back in my room, we took our places in front of the Mirror. I caught my father studying my face.

"I like having my only daughter as my head priestess. It's the only way to be sure no secrets escape," he said.

I bit back the retort. I was angry that he hid things from me, but now was not the time to talk about it.

"Why did you think the boy was the one from the prophecy?" I asked instead. And then, another thought struck me. "You haven't spoken to Raven since his treason, have you?"

My father didn't answer.

Anger boiled inside my chest. "So, you knew exactly what the boy was up to. It was no coincidence that you appeared in my tower when you did."

He grinned. "Very clever, my daughter."

I shivered. "Why didn't you tell me? You knew I couldn't have told the boy anything. And yet, you made me feel guilty. Why?"

He stepped closer. I could feel his cool breath on my cheek.

"Remember, Marya, the first lesson I taught you about separating your feelings. Remember the men who gave their lives to bring you pleasure."

I remembered. How could I forget?

"Come here," my father put his arms around me and pulled me close, cradling me in his embrace. I froze. He'd taught me on my thirteenth birthday to never long for his touch. And yet, I still did. More, I depended on it, on these rare moments when he took me into his arms.

Perhaps it was the magic he used to bind my will to him. I didn't care. These moments were worth everything, worth the tears of the Sacrifice Maidens, the silent obedience of their heartbroken parents, the lonely, loveless nights up in my chamber at the top of the East Tower.

I buried my face in his chest, inhaling his scent like cool

132

moonlit stone, feeling my troubles dissipate as his hands caressed my hair.

"Guilt," my father said against my bent head, "is a good emotion. Guilt and anger. They help you to stay on guard. And you are still on guard, aren't you, Marya?"

"Yes, Father," I breathed out.

"Good."

He ran his hands through my hair and down my back. I shivered.

This is a trick. A trick to take me off guard, to let dangerous feelings slip through. A test.

I might have fallen for it when I was thirteen, but not now. I was calm. I was detached. The only shades of emotions were anger and guilt. No, not even those. I was the Mistress of the Solstice, the head priestess at my father's side. All the longing, all the warmth my treacherous body felt in response to his touch, was no more than a trap my father had laid for me, to test how powerful I had become.

My power was infinite.

I felt my father's hands drop away.

"Good. You have learned your lesson well, Marya. I am glad."

I breathed out, letting the tension go. I felt my hands tremble and clenched them into fists so my father wouldn't see.

"Are you feeling better now, Marya?"

I nodded. I felt weak. I felt like an empty shell, searching for energy to come and fill it.

"The boy is but a tool, brought forth by my enemies to challenge your powers, Marya. He is not acting of his own will. He has none."

I nodded again.

"And now, we will learn his story and see who, or what, is really behind this."

Again, I nodded. I had to do what I must. I had to.

"You are strong, Marya," Kashchey went on. "Because you are different. Always remember that."

"I do, Father," I whispered. "I do."

Anna Kashina

IVAN

Ivan's mind raced. *You'll have to do all the talking.* But Wolf had never mentioned anything about leaving him alone to face Yaga. He was wise, and powerful, and ancient. He was always around. He was supposed to protect Ivan. Right?

"My friend was here just a moment ago," he said. "I'm sure he'll be back any minute. We travel together."

"Your friend is surely smarter than you are." Baba Yaga laughed. "He ran away when he saw you wander into my lair. You're the one who had to stay and do all the silly talking. Teaches you a thing or two, doesn't it?"

It certainly does. "We didn't come here accidentally. We came here looking for you."

"You did, did you?" A spark of interest gleamed in the yellow eyes. "Whatever for?"

Ivan took a deep breath. "I guess if you eat me, you'll never know."

"Oh, no you don't. You're going to tell me everything and then it's the kettle for you, boy."

Ivan smiled. "I won't be the one to argue with you, old mother. Just let me clean your house first. It's too sad to think of an old woman like you living here all alone, with no one to help with the chores. I'll clean up and fix your door, and if my friend doesn't show up with rabbits by the end of it, you can still eat me, right?"

"I suppose," she said. "There's no harm in waiting. If you came out here looking for me like you say, you must know you can't escape unless I let you."

"Of course I know, old mother."

There was a brook nearby and it wasn't hard to persuade

the hut to walk over to it. Thick reeds on its banks made good cleaning rags, and Ivan soon got absorbed in scrubbing, and rinsing, and mending. He liked to do things well. And he'd told the truth—after seeing Baba Yaga crying over a resurrected warrior in the Cat's tale he couldn't believe she was evil. Just lonely, and neglected.

Where had Wolf gone?

He found stems of flax with their tiny blue flowers growing upstream, and wove a bunch of them into a rope. He knew how to set a simple rabbit trap. He and his brothers had done it sometimes, when they'd played in the palace gardens.

Vassily had always said that a real man should be able to feed himself, and not depend on his servants for everything. Little Ivan used to feel sorry for the fluffy rabbits with their beady, frightened eyes, but he believed every word his smart elder brother spoke.

He'd always adored Vassily. Until he'd overheard his brothers one day telling their father how Ivan had mistaken a bull for a stallion and had nearly killed himself riding the angry beast. In truth, it had been Vassily who'd dared Ivan to ride the bull, the same Vassily who had later mocked Ivan in front of their father, making the youngest Tzarevich seem like a fool.

Vassily must have believed Ivan to be too badly hurt to be able to get up and listen at Father's door.

Ivan had never looked at his brothers the same way again, but he did remember everything Vassily had taught him. Including catching rabbits. The skill had come in handy more than once when traveling with Wolf.

He set the trap in the bushes on the other side of the stream and settled on the bank beside the hut, rubbing the kettle with sand. The old metal was already beginning to shine when he heard the cracking sound that signaled a trapped animal.

By the time he was done cleaning, he had six rabbits lying on the grass.

He skinned and gutted them with his knife, cut them into pieces, and filled the kettle from a deeper part of the brook.

Then he washed up and went inside to light the fire.

Baba Yaga had been watching him intently. "You said something about putting fresh grass into my mat."

"Of course," he said. "Just as soon as I start the stew."

He looked around for a spice shelf. The room was hard to recognize. The light of the setting sun shone through the clean window, painting the polished floor boards reddish brown. The mended door fit into its frame without leaving any holes for the mosquitoes to come through. The drapes, still damp, were almost back to their original white, and made the small room seem almost cheery. The merry fire crackled in the stove. The chimney, swept with an old broom found in the corner, didn't smoke anymore, and the logs in the stove gave off the pleasantly heady smell of burning pine.

He found the cabinet with salt and some spices that smelled like they'd be good in the stew. In a corner, he came across a sack of beets, onions, and potatoes. They were beginning to wilt, but he judged them good enough for cooking. Then he went outside to pick some grass for the mat.

The clearing was awash in the last orange beams of the sun. In its light Ivan saw a dark shape sitting in the grass by the forest hedge.

"You!" He strode over to Wolf's side, relief washing over him. "I was beginning to get worried. Where have you been?"

Wolf just sat there, staring past Ivan.

A rustle of grass made Ivan turn around.

Baba Yaga stood by the door, arms crossed over her chest. "So, that's your friend, eh? I can see now why he was so hard to find!"

Ivan stepped back. Why was Wolf silent? What was wrong?

Baba Yaga limped slightly, but despite her ancient looks, her walk was as energetic as that of a young woman. She no longer looked disheveled. Ivan wasn't sure when she had a chance to change and clean up, but her graying hair was tidily braided and tucked away into a clean linen dress, with an apron tied on top. In fact, she no longer looked that old either—a respectable, middle-aged matron with the remains of a majestic beauty set deeply into her fine-boned face.

It seemed to Ivan that as she walked across the glade she and Wolf were having an inaudible conversation. Then she reached the beast and stopped in front of him, her arms once again crossed over her chest.

"So," she said. "You dare show your ugly, hairy muzzle here? You are no longer afraid of my wrath?"

Wolf growled. Ivan once again became acutely aware of how similar were Wolf's eyes and the eyes of Baba Yaga.

"Silent?" She seemed even younger now, slender like a village maiden. "No voice left, eh?"

Wolf growled again and lowered his head.

She cocked her head, her face lighting up with a smile. "So, you really are mute. Wordless, like the beast you are."

Wolf raised his head. Their eyes locked—yellow to yellow. There was a conversation going on in their gazes. Watching them made Ivan feel like an intruder.

Then Baba Yaga stirred. "Boy! Bring me that old axe you found behind the stove. A beast, such as he is, doesn't deserve to be killed with a decent weapon."

Ivan didn't move. After a moment she turned, her angry glance forcing him to step back. "You dare defy me, kettle meat?"

Ivan swallowed. "Wolf is my friend, and whatever spell has made him lose his speech, he is no ordinary beast. I will not let you harm him, old mother."

Her vertical pupils narrowed to slits. Her gaze stung. "You dare speak on his behalf?"

It took all of Ivan's courage to hold her gaze. "I do, old mother. Whatever the reason for his silence, whatever has come between the two of you in the past, he is all I have in the world and I will stand by him."

"All you have in this world, boy?" She leaned toward Ivan. "What kind of an outcast are you?"

Ivan shifted from foot to foot. He'd never articulated how he felt about Wolf, but what he'd said was true. Wolf had become his only true friend in the whole world. He would not let this old woman mistreat his friend.

It crossed his mind that, powerful as she was, there was nothing he could do to stop her, but he dismissed the unhelpful thought.

"It's my fault we came here, old mother. I messed up. Wolf agreed to help me out. He wouldn't be here if I hadn't been so foolish, so if you need to punish someone, it would be me."

Baba Yaga sighed and lowered her arms. "You must have a real power to bring out the goodness in people, boy. Otherwise, how could I see this monster and not smash both of you to pieces like I should?"

Wolf looked at her in silence, his tension betrayed only by the knots of tight muscle that made his thick gray fur bristle at the neck.

Baba Yaga laughed. "Now I know why your faithful companion left you all alone to face my wrath. And, you are brave indeed to face me for the sake of this unworthy creature. Perhaps he still has a grain of good in him, to inspire such devotion."

Her gaze lost some of its iron. Ivan stirred, as if the bonds that had held him in place were suddenly loosened.

"Perhaps," he ventured, "we can all sit around and eat some rabbit stew? There's plenty for everyone."

Baba Yaga stared at him. Ivan suppressed an urge to cower under the yellow flame of her stare. Yet, at length her gaze softened, and the set of her jaw eased a bit.

"I can't decide if you're daft or clever. Whichever way it is, you're truly something else."

She turned and made her way back into the hut.

Ivan and Wolf exchanged glances. After a moment's hesitation Ivan turned to follow the old woman. At length, he heard the shuffle of paws following him through the grass.

MARYA

"**S**how me Ivan," I commanded the Mirror.

The mist of the polished surface thinned to reveal a shape crawling through thick grass. It was hard to tell whether he was anywhere near the Hidden Stream.

"What do you think?" my father asked.

I scoffed. "An ordinary fool." Seen like this, the boy indeed looked like a common villager. Perhaps all the talk of the prophecy was making us see things that weren't there?

"Perhaps you're right. Yet, Leshy and the Net were no accident. Someone is helping him."

"The father of some unfortunate maid you kidnapped?"

"Why involve ourselves in guesswork? Let's see for ourselves."

"All right." I turned to the Mirror. "Show us how Ivan came to our kingdom."

The Mirror grew dim and light again, picking up the story from where I'd left it last, as Ivan was riding out of his kingdom. His horse was truly a disaster. No beast of any magic, for sure.

Uneventful days flashed in the Mirror like moments as Ivan rode, following a trail that led out of their kingdom to the east. He crossed the border of the Fourteenth kingdom, and into a deep forest.

The Thirty Ninth kingdom can be reached from the Twelfth Kingdom by riding east for something like...a year, I believe? That is, if you don't encounter any obstacles on the way.

The first of the obstacles came in the shape of a crossroads with a huge boulder planted right in the middle of it. The Mirror showed us the inscription on the boulder, made in runic letters. It said:

Come thou straight, and let thyself and thy mount be starved.
Come thou right, and lose thy mount.
Come thou left, and lose thy life.
Turn thou back, and go in peace.

By the looks of it, it must have been written very long ago.

I found myself wishing for Ivan to turn back. Really, whatever his quest, it couldn't be worth the trouble.

His next logical choice was to go right and, in spite of the complete uselessness of his horse, Ivan hesitated before making that decision. He actually made a move to go straight, but reasonably decided against it.

He turned right and followed the disappearing path deeper and deeper into the woods. Judging by its state, not many traveling knights ever made it down here, and of those few, even fewer decided to go on after seeing the stone.

The path Ivan followed soon ended in a glade, covered in scattered horse bones, some of them years old. We watched Ivan dismount and walk around the glade trying to find where the trail lead from there.

We saw his horse suddenly panic and jump away from something that appeared like lightning and landed straight on the horse's back. A huge gray beast. It growled, aiming at the panicked horse's neck, and in seconds Ivan's unfortunate mount fell to the ground, squealing and kicking its legs in the air before finally going still.

The gray beast lifted its head, looking at Ivan's horrified face, and the Mirror turned the view around to let us look straight at its blood-stained snout.

I heard my father gasp even as I echoed the sound myself.

"The Gray Wolf," my father whispered.

I shivered. One of the oldest creatures that ever lived, the Gray Wolf was one of the Primals, like Bayun the Cat. Everyone, including the Immortals, feared Primal magic, a mysterious form of power no creature, living or undead, could resist. Even the worst of our kin thought it best to stay out of his path.

Ivan was likely the only one in the area apparently oblivious to this knowledge. Not only did he show no reverence at the sight of the great beast, but he actually reached for his sword and would have drawn it if the wolf in the Mirror hadn't produced a sound more or less resembling human laughter.

"Put that thing away, boy. You'll only hurt yourself."

"Why did you kill my horse?" Ivan demanded.

I held my breath. I shivered at the thought of what might happen to Ivan after addressing Wolf in such a disrespectful way.

But the beast was apparently in a forgiving mood.

"Did you read the sign?"

"What sign?"

"On the boulder over there." Wolf sat on the ground and scratched his ear in a dog-like gesture. He was huge, his head in a sitting positing coming up nearly to Ivan's shoulder. "Oh, don't tell me your parents never taught you to read. What do they teach you traveling knights these days, anyway?" He threw a longing glance at the horse carcass, clearly looking forward to a meal.

Ivan lifted his chin. "I can read as well as anyone. Of course, I read the sign."

"Maybe you don't know your left from your right?" Wolf spoke with exaggerated patience, as if talking to a little child.

For the first time Ivan looked doubtful. "You mean... Did you write that inscription on the boulder?"

"Thank the stars. Finally!"

"But..."

Wolf sighed. "The horse was your mount, right?"

"Yes..."

"There you have it!" Wolf triumphantly bared his teeth and took a step toward the horse.

Ivan watched him circle his dead prey, as if forgetting all about Ivan.

"But what am I supposed to do without a horse?" he asked after a pause.

"Why should I care?" Wolf growled.

"You should care because you killed my horse."

"Arrrgggggghhhhhh!" The wolf's growl flattened the leaves of the trees, and rippled outward. Even the walls in my room trembled.

Ivan jumped away, keeping his hands in front of him in a calming gesture. "Just tell me what I should do next, all right?" he asked in a soothing voice.

Wolf licked his muzzle. "I suppose that's the only way to get rid of you. I could have eaten you, you know, but I have to respect the inscription on the boulder. A pact is a pact. Just go east. You'll reach a village in two days."

Ivan turned and walked out of sight.

I unclenched my hands that had balled into fists without me realizing it, and stretched my fingers surreptitiously.

I was confused. It took either extreme courage, or extreme foolishness to face the Gray Wolf the way Ivan had. His innocent blue eyes made it hard for me to decide which. It was hard to imagine that this boy possessed so much courage. Did his real strength lie in deception?

The scene in the Mirror changed again to show the Tzar's palace in the Twelfth Kingdom. I recognized Vassily, whose eyes hadn't lost their calculating look. He sat at a table, dressed in a rich royal *caftan*—red and gold, quite appropriate, and very becoming, for an heir to the throne. It took me longer to recognize Fedor. He'd grown up fat and sloppy, and his face wore a perpetual look of boredom. I felt distantly sorry for Fedor. He could have been different if he'd grown up in a better place.

Vassily spoke to a man dressed in simple peasant garb, but with the look and posture of a warrior. I wondered if everyone could see through the disguise as well as I did.

"He is riding east. Follow him. Soon after the border of the Fourteenth Kingdom you will find a boulder at the crossroads with words on it; never mind what they say."

Of course. The man couldn't read. Not uncommon.

"Most of the people at this boulder turn back," Vassily went on. "If Ivan does, you and your men will meet him on your way. If not, he would go right. Father didn't give him much of a horse." He grinned. "Ivan would think nothing of parting with it."

"Parting with the horse?" the man in the peasant outfit asked. "Why?"

"Never mind that," Vassily snapped. "Turn right, but don't go too far. You'll probably see the fool wandering around on foot. Whatever you do, don't go into the glade that opens out from the woods."

"But why?"

"There are beasts in the glade. They attack any horse that enters the glade. I expect Ivan will lose his, by the time you get there. Without his horse he cannot go far. He should be easy prey for you and your men."

Prey? But what possible threat could Ivan be to you?

Did Vassily suspect his youngest brother capable of becoming a hero? Was he also a victim of Ivan's deception?

"This bag holds one hundred gold pieces," Vassily said, handing the man a sizeable leather pouch. "You will get another one like it when you bring me his signet ring. But make sure he's dead before you take it. If you lie to me, I will find you anywhere you go and make you regret the day you were born, do you hear?"

"Yes, master. I will do as you ask."

I felt caught up in this string of events, just as I'd been caught before, just as I so easily lost myself in Ivan's smile and the warmth of his shining blue eyes. I was torn. I didn't know whether to wish him dead or alive. And I couldn't possibly take my eyes off the Mirror.

My father seemed no less absorbed in the story than I.

The hired killers—five of them—had no difficulty catching up with Ivan who, first on his poor horse, and then on foot, couldn't travel very fast. I tried to feel nothing as I watched them run him down on their horses and then dismount to finish the job with their swords. The leader took something off his hand—the ring, no doubt—and the five of them left, riding west.

Nobody could survive that.

It was the Gray Wolf who came to his aid. He jumped out of the bushes as soon as the killers had gone. Ivan looked quite dead to me, but the wolf apparently thought otherwise. He tore off the bloodied strips of Ivan's shirt, then chewed some leaves and spat them on Ivan's wounds. He put his hairy snout, still covered with dried horse-blood, over Ivan's mouth to help him breathe. He felt for Ivan's heart with his paw and then his eyes sparkled with something very similar to human joy. And then, with effort, he dragged Ivan up onto his own back and carried him all the way to a village, where he dropped him near somebody's threshold and disappeared.

Events in the Mirror flashed by much more quickly than in real life. The man who found Ivan on his doorstep—Nikifor the Herb Man—turned out to be the most skilled healer in the nearby kingdoms. An old man with sad eyes, his sleek hands seemingly able to carry out virtually any task. He did wonders for Ivan, mending his gaping wounds, feeding him with broth and herb stews, holding endless vigils by his bed-side listening to Ivan's strained breath and barely perceptible heartbeat.

Bringing a man back from death.

Quite likely, Nikifor was the only person in all the king-doms who could have saved Ivan's life. The Grey Wolf had gone to great lengths to make sure the boy lived. But why?

Before long, Ivan was able to get up, and a bit later to walk outside and sit in the sunshine with his host and savior. He became a welcome guest in the lonely man's *izba*, and helped with the chores around the house. Then, one day, the Grey Wolf came back.

The cascade of images in the Mirror slowed.

The picture became so real that I could almost feel the heat of the crackling firewood in Nikifor's cozy room, and smell the drying herbs hanging from the ceiling.

We were about to see the essence of our question.

I held my breath as the gray beast entered the small *izba*

145

and settled on the mat by the stove. As he spoke, his voice echoed through the small wooden building and through the Mirror, into the large stone space of my room.

"Go out, boy," Wolf said to Ivan. "Get some firewood."

He and Nikifor exchanged looks. Ivan, however, didn't move.

"Glad to see you, too," he said.

I shivered. Would the boy ever learn to show proper respect to the Primals?

Wolf obviously wasn't in the mood. "*Now,*" he growled.

Nikifor flinched, and even I suppressed the urge to step back. But Ivan showed no fear.

"I am well, thank you," he replied calmly.

The two stared at each other. Then the beast settled back by the fire. "I see."

Nikifor nodded, his eyes on Ivan lighting up with quiet pride. "You were right all along."

Wolf turned to the old man. "Have you meddled in something you weren't supposed to?"

"No, I spoke of nothing to the boy."

"Then, why does he defy me?"

"I do not," Ivan said. "I just think that I have the right to be part of your conversation. I know you came here to talk about me."

"How could you possibly know that?" Wolf growled.

Ivan smiled. "I could see it, in the way you looked at me just now. Besides, why else would you be sending me outside?"

My skin prickled. Not daft then. And then I realized this with terrifying clarity. Daftness was his weapon. It made people underestimate him.

Just like I did.

Great Kupalo, what trouble did we get into?

Wolf fixed Ivan with a stare that made me suppress a gasp. The beast's Primal force was enormous. Was the boy immune to it?

"It only concerns you if I say so." Wolf growled in Ivan's

face "Nobody gave you permission to speak. *Meat*."

He threw the last word through clenched teeth. It stung. Ivan's hands balled into fists that turned his knuckles white. Yet, his voice was still calm.

"You ate my horse," he said. "Had you not, I wouldn't have been here at all."

"Perhaps," Wolf said. "I doubt, however, that your horse would have saved you from the killers your brother set on your trail. There were five of them, and their horses were worlds better than yours, boy."

"Perhaps, but that doesn't give you, or anyone else, the right to decide my life for me."

Wolf studied him for a moment. "Have you ever been part of a prophecy, boy?"

"Prophecies don't work," Ivan said. "Everyone knows that."

There was another pause.

"They do. They work, if you make them. And, as it happens, there is one I intend to see fulfilled. It involves a certain Kashchey of the Thirty Ninth kingdom."

Ivan lifted his head.

"That interests you, doesn't it? Kashchey's demands on your kingdom make it your business, like it or not."

"You mean my brother's kingdom," Ivan said.

"Your homeland. Your people. Many kingdoms pay tribute to this monster who calls himself 'immortal'. Do you know what he does to those who cannot pay? Or perhaps you'd rather your kingdom fell, like others have?"

"Why do the affairs of my kingdom concern you, Wolf?"

Wolf and Nikifor exchanged long glances. It seemed to me as if they were continuing a conversation from before. Obviously one held without Ivan, otherwise we would have seen it in the Mirror.

"We all have our own interests," Wolf said. "Nikifor does. And, even if you think you owe me nothing, boy, you still owe Nikifor for bringing you back."

Ivan turned to the old man. "That I do. A debt hard to repay."

The old man shook his head. "I am not asking you for anything, boy. I am a healer. Gods know, I would have done all I could for you, debt or not. It's just that you are... so right for it."

"What is your interest in this, old father?"

Nikifor's face became sad. "I lived in Kashchey's kingdom once. A long time ago." His face froze, so that for a moment it seemed to me as if some magic had turned him to stone. "I had a daughter back then," he said, his voice barely audible. "Svetlana." He paused and clenched his hands.

I felt nausea clutch my throat as a suspicion where this was going crept into my head. *Svetlana.* She would have been before my time.

The old man swallowed and continued in a steady voice. "She was twelve when our small village was selected to provide a maiden for the Solstice Sacrifice. The Chosen Maiden—Fiokla—was the daughter of the village elder. On the morning the Mistress came for her, Fiokla was nowhere to be found. And then, her father finally appeared, dragging the girl by the arm."

The old man paused, clenching his long, pale fingers.

"Fiokla's father was red with embarrassment. As was the maiden herself. It turned out that, learning of her fate, she ran off with the miller's son and spilled her virginal blood."

I sighed. Such things happened. Some maidens, or even their families, just couldn't accept their fate. Not often, since the man who served to defile the Sacrifice Maiden was seized and executed, but the maiden herself was spared. On such occasions the Mistress of the Solstice then picked another suitable maiden from those in the chosen village.

I didn't want to listen to the old man's story. Yet, I strained to catch his every word.

"My Svetlana was the oldest virgin left in our village. The others were all children, so even though she was only twelve, she was the only possible choice. By rules, we had to give her up in Fiokla's stead."

For a while there was no sound but the creaking of the fire

in the stove.

"She was all I had," Nikifor said. "She did not have to die." His hands trembled and he clenched them into fists. "On that day I swore an oath to do all I can to bring ruin to their evil cult of Kupalo."

I felt disturbed. How could this man presume to judge our God? Sad or unfair as his fate had been, how could he put his petty family affairs on the same scale as the greater good?

"And you?" Ivan asked Wolf. "What is your interest in all this?"

Wolf sighed, measuring Ivan up and down with his gaze.

"You will learn of it, if I deem you worthy, boy. And now— show me your birthmark."

This time the power of his voice smothered any possible argument. Ivan reached over and pulled off his shirt.

I covered my mouth, as if the people in the Mirror could actually hear my gasp.

A hero of legend comes marked by an arrow through turmoil and gloom. An arrow-shaped birthmark. It was there, on his left shoulder, as if painted on the skin with reddish-gold dye. It pointed diagonally down, more or less at the heart.

Wolf nodded. "Impressive, isn't it?"

"Wait," Ivan protested. "You don't think I'm the chosen one or something?"

Wolf snorted, suppressing a laugh. "You should be old enough to know, boy. There are no 'chosen ones'. You'll do, that's all."

"What if I don't want to?"

"As if you have something better to do."

"And you won't even tell me why *you* want this to come about?"

"Some day. Perhaps."

"Enough," my father said beside me. The Mirror filled with mist, hiding all from view.

I stepped away, my heart beating like a bird in a cage. I'd always thought the affairs of our kingdom were our own. I never knew there were people out there who wished to destroy our worship of Kupalo.

"Why did you stop, Father?" I asked.

"I heard enough," he said. "Another feeble attempt to make the prophecy come true. We'll crush this boy like we did the others."

"But what is Wolf's part in this?" I asked. "Why does he care?"

My father looked at me. For the first time in my life, I saw fear in his eyes.

"Come, Marya. You must have your herb drink and go to sleep. You need to replenish your powers. And I have something else to do."

"What, Father?"

He looked me in the eye. "I think I know who else helped this boy. But I must be sure."

"Can I help?" I asked, disturbed by an expression in his face I couldn't quite read.

"Not this time, Marya." He took me in his arms and caressed my hair, running his hands down through the smooth, thick strands. This time there was no challenge in this. Instead, his touch engulfed me in an aura of calm. I inhaled his scent, so familiar and comforting, the cold scent of stone washed by full moon that symbolized the safety of the walls that enclosed me from the turmoil and passions of the outside world. The stone of my father's world around me.

"Rest, my sweet Marya," he said. "Your father will set things right."

IVAN

Baba Yaga pushed her empty bowl away and leaned back against the warm stove.

"For what this beast did," she said to Ivan, though she watched Wolf, "there's no forgiveness. Yet, there is nothing to be done. I would have killed him, but all I could do was kill his gift of human speech. And only when I was around. To each his own."

Ivan waited, but there was nothing else. He longed to ask her what Wolf had done to make her so angry, but he knew it was useless. Besides, it seemed best not to disturb the past.

"So," he said, "you will not help?"

"Him—no." Baba Yaga slid her gaze over Wolf and turned away. "I know he thinks he can undo the evil he has caused, but there is no going back. And revenge, however sweet, solves nothing. I will not go along with it."

"What about helping *me*?"

Baba Yaga got up from the table and limped over to the corner behind the stove. She looked older again, a grandmother entertaining guests in her lonely hut. There was a clanking as she rummaged in the dark depths. A furry shape darted along the wall and disappeared into a crack under the stove. It looked bigger than a normal mouse and Ivan could have sworn it had more than four legs.

He looked away.

After a while Baba Yaga pulled out a dusty vial. It looked darker than the one in the Cat's tale, but Ivan recognized it at once. She held it up to the light and shook it.

"Empty," she said. "That boy, Ilia, took a lot to come back to life. The fool managed to get his head severed, you know."

151

Ivan remembered the tears in her eyes, real human tears rolling down the parched skin of her immortal face. *She's lonely. An old lonely woman with ancient powers, who will never die.*

She sat down and put the vial on the table. Wolf eyed it warily.

"To you mortals the Water brings life," she said. "But we Immortals can never touch a single drop of it. Perhaps this is why the Stream never reveals itself to a mortal. There should be a balance in everything."

Ivan picked up the vial and shook it gently. There wasn't anything left in it. Not even a drop.

"Will you tell me the song?" he asked.

"Useless, boy. The Stream will never reveal itself to you. Besides, you'll never make it in time."

"I have to try,"

"But why? To her—to Marya—this is but a fancy. She doesn't need the Water to bring life. She just wanted to give you, silly boy, an impossible task."

"This isn't about me," Ivan said. "It is about Kashchey and the power of Kupalo. If I fulfill her task, I will have a chance to put an end to the whole Solstice tradition in this kingdom. There will be no virgin sacrifice and Kashchey's subjects will see him for what he truly is. Don't you see? It could put an end to Kashchey's rule."

"Perhaps," Baba Yaga said. "At one point all I wanted to do is wriggle all life out of his miserable form. But that time is long gone. Hurting Kashchey won't undo the past."

She seemed to address these words to the wolf, whose eyes glowed out of the corner of the room like jewels. A charge passed between them, as if, despite his muteness, they spoke to one another.

Then she stirred and looked back at Ivan.

"So, you will not help?" Ivan asked again.

She shook her head. "The lives of these maidens mean nothing to me, boy."

No, because you haven't seen any of them. None of them had a chance to touch your heart. Not like Wolf, who somehow hurt you enough that you made him speechless; not like Ilia, who you brought back to life only to see him leave you and go his own way.

He raised his head and met the look in her yellow eyes.

"What did Ilia's life mean to you? What has he done to make you travel all the way out to the ends of the world and risk your life to gather the sacred water?"

She stared back, unblinking. The silence rustled with the creaky fire, squeaked with the strange creatures hiding in the thatched corners of the chicken-legged house.

"He was perhaps even younger than you," she finally said. "And he had this fire in his eyes, like he knew something no one else did, like he was going to set things right for everybody in the world. A promising lad, I thought. So, when I saw him, lifeless, his pretty head cut away from his body, it seemed like such a silly waste. I—"

She fell silent again. They sat for a while, subsumed in the quiet sounds of the living house.

"The girl they will sacrifice this year," Ivan said, "is called Alyona. She is sixteen, the youngest daughter in a family of six. She has four elder sisters and a younger brother. When she dies, her soul will merge with Kashchey's to keep him young for another year. He will devour her, as he has many others before her, and every time it happens, he grows in power, so that he can control more lands and conjure more troops to invade other kingdoms. Soon, his power will grow so great that no one in the world will be able to resist him."

"And you propose to stop all this?" There was amusement in Baba Yaga's voice.

"I have to try. Every year he becomes more powerful than before. This year it may still be possible. Next year, it may be too late."

"You speak nobly, but I have lived too long in this world to believe noble words. You are much like Ilia, but he was foolish and you, I know, are no fool. What is it that really drives you, boy?"

He met her gaze. *There is no reason to deny it,* he told himself. *No reason at all.*

"Last year," he said, "our kingdom received a messenger from Kashchey. We are to submit to his rule and pay tribute to his kingdom. If we refuse, he will destroy our crops and lay our lands to waste."

She laughed. "Don't tell me that you *care*. Your kingdom cast you out. Your brothers sent killers after you and nearly succeeded. You owe them nothing."

"Not them," Ivan said. "I owe it to my people. No matter what my father thinks of me, I am still a tzar's son and I am responsible for my kingdom's well-being."

She shook her head. "Noble words. But empty. No one puts others before himself, boy. No one. If you think you do, you are merely fooling yourself. Don't tell me I was wrong about you and you're a fool after all."

"You are right about me." He smiled. "I am not a fool. I am thinking only of myself. In all my travels, the only thought that keeps me strong is the thought that my home always lies behind, just the way I left it. I cannot bear to lose that. And if I have to risk my life to keep this feeling, I will gladly do it. For if my homeland goes to waste, there will be truly nothing left for me in the world."

She looked at him for a long time. Flickers from the fire danced in her yellow eyes.

"You're even crazier than Ilia was," she said thoughtfully. "I always told Kashchey that one day his hunger for power will bring about his doom. He can easily control normal people, true. But sooner or later one of you crazy ones will run across his path and leave him with no escape."

Wolf stirred in his corner. His eyes caught the firelight and glowed like two coals. He bared his teeth.

"What is it?" Baba Yaga asked.

The beast got up and walked over to Ivan. Silently he grabbed the corner of Ivan's collar and pulled. The thin linen tore.

"Hey!" Ivan exclaimed, jumping to his feet. "That was my best shirt! Why have you—"

Baba Yaga stared. She wasn't looking at Ivan's face. Her eyes were fixed on his left shoulder. Just above the heart.

Even the hut stopped its squeaking and rustling as if the house, too, had a pair of eyes fixed on Ivan.

"I see," Baba Yaga said slowly.

"What?" Ivan asked. Nikifor the Healer had looked at him in the same way, when the man had first seen the gaping wound in Ivan's chest. The power of that look had caught him up on death's doorstep. And now, this look made him shiver.

"Why didn't you two tell me?" Baba Yaga asked Wolf.

Wolf gave her a look.

"Sorry," she waved her hand. "Never mind that."

She got up and started rummaging around the hut. From a dark corner she produced an old beaten broom.

"You stay here, boy," she said. "I won't be long."

She grabbed the empty vial off the table and stuck in into her apron pocket.

"Where are you going?"

"To get you the Water, of course," she snapped. "Don't be a fool, boy. Fools waste their time with silly questions, and time is too precious to waste. You only have three days before the Solstice, am I right?"

"Yes," Ivan said, dazed. "But why—why did you change your mind?"

"You were eloquent enough to convince me. And this is all you will hear from me. If you want to know more, ask your four-legged friend here. Although, if he hasn't told you already, he probably won't tell you now. I'll be back before dawn. Don't even think of sleeping on my *lezhanka*. You can make a bed for yourself over there on the floor. Don't mind the furry ones—they don't bite. Normally, at least."

She leaned out of the doorway and whistled through her teeth. The wave of sound flattened the grass on the glade and rippled the water in the brook. Ivan's ears went numb. Dazed, he watched a giant wooden mortar stumble into the glade and come to a standstill in front of the hut's open door.

With broom in hand, Baba Yaga clambered in and tucked her dress neatly into the mortar's opening.

"Can I go with you?" Ivan asked from the doorway.

"Don't be a fool, boy," she snapped. "The Stream doesn't reveal itself to mortals, remember? How exceptional do you think you are?"

She swept the air with her broom. The wind, raised by the motion, whistled through the glade. The hut's door banged against the logs of the wall. The hinges wailed.

The mortar lifted off and was gone in a cloud of dust.

"Thank you," Ivan called after her.

He turned and walked back into the hut, carefully closing the door behind him.

"Now," Wolf said. It was so unexpected to hear his voice after the long silence that Ivan jumped. "Let's go and catch some more rabbits. The old hag'll be hungry when she comes back. You don't want to end up in her kettle."

"I thought we were past that,"

"You think too much, boy. Move. Go."

"How is it that you didn't tell me about your curse before we came here?" Ivan asked following Wolf out onto grass damp with evening dew.

"I did tell you," Wolf snapped. "You just didn't listen, as always."

Ivan sighed. Wolf did say Ivan would have to do all the talking. If he'd understood what that meant, though, he could perhaps have prepared better. But, it was useless to argue with Wolf. Besides, it hardly mattered anymore.

The wolf's gray tail blended with the shadows on the far side of the brook. Then came the sound of cracking, and a short squeak. A moment later Wolf reappeared, a limp furry shape hanging from his mouth.

"One," Wolf said, laying the kill at Ivan's feet. "Get yourself busy. We'll need at least nine this time."

Ivan sighed and settled down to clean the meat.

MARYA

My dream tonight was much more vivid. Except when I stepped through the forest hedge to enter the glade by the Sacrifice Pool, it was suddenly dark, and although the man turned to face me, I could not make out his features in the dim light. Then, we were no longer by the Sacrifice Pool, but in my chamber. He was in front of me, beckoning. Unsure, as if sleepwalking, I followed him to the dark quadrangle of my bed that I could sense more than see in the depths of the circular room. I longed to see his face, I was not afraid anymore, but all I could see was a pale oval in a frame of black hair.

"You must sleep now," he whispered, and I felt his hands search for the ties that undid my dress, I felt the silky cloth slide down my shoulders, sweep across the skin of my stomach and thighs, and collapse in a heap around my feet. I felt his hands run along my naked body in a way that made my skin rise in goosebumps. This was not the touch of a man who wanted to soothe me to sleep. This was the touch of arousal, and my body responded to it.

Part of my mind wanted to protest, but another, stronger part, longed for this closeness. I gave in to the excitement, ready for whatever was to come.

He took his hands off me and stepped forward to turn down the cover of my bedding for me. I slid under it. And then, he took off his garments and slid under the covers after me.

I opened my mouth to speak, but his hand covered my lips, stifling the words. His face was so close that it almost touched mine. His breath was cool but it burned me as he whispered:

"Hush, my sweet Marya. You must relax now."

I shivered as I felt the smoothness of his bare skin next to mine, the closeness of his body. Something about it was unthinkable, yet in some other way it seemed right. Unable to control myself, I sank into his arms, feeling that I belonged there, in this embrace that was better than the caresses of all the lovers in the world.

My burning body yielded to the touch of his cool hands with the thirst of a wanderer stranded in a desert. My mind, a separate entity at the edge of my consciousness, screamed something that I didn't want to hear. I let it go, I shooed it away like a bothersome fly. I gave in to the bliss no man in the world could give me.

Until now.

My arms reached out in response to his caress, but he gently pressed them down to my sides. He whispered in my ear, but I couldn't hear the words. Only the coolness of his breath, the way it touched my burning skin, bringing a tension that coiled inside me until it broke loose in intense desire.

My mind circled somewhere above, flapping its silly wings.

His hands drove me to the edge of ecstasy and kept me hovering there until I could feel my body no longer. I was all ecstasy, a pure essence held together only by my lover's immense skill. Just a little more and my ecstasy would be released and I would disappear.

I longed for it. I wanted us to become one, stone and moonlight, coldness and fire, but he skillfully held me at the edge, touching me with nothing but his hands, his whispers in my ear sweet, senseless and tender like a lover's talk.

Once I opened my eyes and saw him, his onyx-black eyes glowing in his pale face, indistinct in the darkness of my chamber. He leaned forward and kissed my eyes closed, but as I searched for his lips with my hungry mouth, they were gone.

I wished he would ravage me like my father did with his women, satisfy his wild passion for young pretty flesh on me. I knew he wanted it too, for his hands faltered in their controlled movements and he held me in an embrace that was no longer designed to please me, but to quench his own thirst. And then, as his passion echoed through me, as I felt his quivering muscles, his manhood pressed tight against my body, I finally came undone, my ecstasy releasing itself in a surge of such power that for an endless instant I forgot who I was.

I did not remember what came later, or how he finally left me, dazed, empty of every feeling except my devotion to this man and his greater cause. *I am Marya, Mistress of the Solstice, daughter of Kashchey the Immortal, the best man in the whole world.* With that thought, I sank into a deep sleep...

The dream went on. Again, I walked to the Sacrifice Pool and again I saw the dark man sitting, crouched by the water. But this time a feeling of joy engulfed me and I stepped through the forest hedge and called out to him, my lover.

He turned his head.

It was Kashchey.

My mind screamed in agony, but I smiled.

His lips smiled in return, but his eyes were cold.

Once again, I forced my mind to retreat and gave in to the happiness of seeing him here. It overwhelmed me, leaving no room for cold. I ran to meet him. He jumped up and lifted me in his arms, circling the glade with me.

I wanted to hold him, but I could not. I held something important clenched in my hand, though I did not know what it was.

I searched for a place to put it down, but Kashchey stroked my body with such passion that I forgot.

"I was waiting for you, my love," he whispered.

He lay me gently on the grass and stretched next to me. My heart quivered with bliss as I watched him undo the strings of my dress until his hand found its way inside to caress my swelling breasts.

"Someone will see us," I whispered. "We should go inside."

He leaned over me and this time there was a smile in his onyx-black eyes.

"No one ever comes to these woods," he said. "And I can't

wait. I want you now!"

He pulled my dress open all the way, leaving me naked below the sky.

I closed my eyes and gave myself to the touch of his hands. The forest stood still around us and the slow river followed its endless course.

There was nobody else in the world.

Nothing else mattered.

The strange, oval object I had been clenching in my hand rolled out of my open palm and disappeared in the tall grass. It rolled to the edge of the water and I heard a splash as it disappeared into the amber depth of the lake.

I never learned what it was.

As I opened my eyes, I saw Praskovia standing by my bed. It was very early, but the first beams of the morning sun had already crept in through the narrow stone window.

The day of the Solstice.

The longest day of the year.

As Praskovia handed me my morning drink, I saw her hands tremble as they clenched the clay mug. I sat in my bed and sipped the hot herb brew, studying my handwoman.

Her face was pale and her eyes red. If I didn't know her better, I would have thought she was crying.

"Praskovia?" I asked handing her back the empty mug.

"Yes, Mistress."

"Are you feeling well?"

"Yes, Mistress."

I stood up and pulled my silky black dress over my head.

"You can't fool me, you know." I peered into her eyes. "You must tell me what's wrong."

For the first time in memory, she avoided my gaze.

I heard wings flap behind me as Raven flew in through the open window.

"Leave her alone, Marya," he said. "She's under orders."

"Whose orders?"

"Your father's."

"She is my handwoman," I said, angry. "What business does my father have to give her orders to hide things from me?"

Raven flew over to a stone ledge to face me.

"What did you and your father do last night?" he asked.

"We—we looked in the Mirror to find out more about the boy. Just like you suggested." I felt something stir at the back of my mind, but I dismissed it. What did last night have to do with it?

"And then?"

"My father left and I went to sleep." I felt treacherous color creep up to my cheeks. My dreams. Surely, Raven couldn't know them, could he?

"Where did he go?"

I opened my mouth and stopped. *Your father will set things right*, he had said. He also said he knew who else was helping the boy, besides the Gray Wolf.

I knew my father all too well.

"What did my father do?" I demanded. *What has he done?*

"He found the one to blame."

"Who?"

"No," Praskovia said. "Stop it. You mustn't know, Mistress. Please."

Chills crept up my spine.

"You will do that, Praskovia?" Raven said. "You will choose Kashchey over your own fa—"

"Stop it, I said!" Praskovia exclaimed. It was a command. But, more than that, it was a plea.

"Your own... father?" I whispered.

Praskovia was suddenly busy, walking over to my trunk and reaching in to rummage inside.

"Come, Mistress," she said. "It's a big day. You must be ready."

"But—"

"It's her choice, Marya," Raven said. "You can't interfere."

"It seems that I can, since my father is involved." I pushed

Praskovia aside and strode out of the room.

The servants' frightened glances led me away from my father's chambers, which were empty, down the narrow stairway to the side of the castle, and eventually, after much searching, down another flight of spiral staircase that seemed as if it would never end, into the damp, moldy space underneath the castle.

The dungeons. I had only been there once in my entire life and I didn't cherish the experience.

I took a burning torch out of its sconce and followed a winding passageway toward a flickering light far ahead. The cold dampness encompassed me with the smell of decay. In the uneven shadows, the walls seemed to creep with things I didn't want to think about.

Down here, I was no longer powerful. I was a frightened young girl, just like the first time I'd wandered here, when I was ten and saw things that I had been told to forget—an order I found impossible to follow.

The stone walls opened into a larger space. A torch flickered in the corner, throwing uneven light onto a dark cloaked figure—my father?—and something else...

I edged forward, the torch suddenly heavy in my weakening hand.

My father turned. "Marya? What are you—"

I looked past him at the old man sprawled on the wall. His arms and legs, spread wide apart, were pinned to the stone by crude iron daggers, surrounded by black splotches of dried blood. His long white hair and thin straight beard were disheveled, his bare chest splayed with blood that almost hid the gashes beneath. His face was so pale it seemed more gray than the stone behind him. Yet his eyes, blue like waters in a summer lake, shone brighter than jewels on his drawn face. The man's body was broken, but his spirit was still intact.

"Release him, Father," I whispered.

"Who told you?" my father demanded. "It's Praskovia, isn't it? I'll have that woman—"

"You will not, Father," I said. "You will release this man

163

and let my servants see to his wounds. And, you will leave Praskovia alone. She told me nothing. I was looking for you and I found you here, that's all."

"This man helped the boy get to your tower. He told the boy about your traps. He also told the boy that we cannot harm him if he asks for your hand. He gave our enemy *weapons* against us!"

I shook my head. "Torturing this man won't undo what he's done. Release him, Father. Do it *now*."

"You can't give me orders, Marya."

"Today," I said, "is the Summer Solstice. The day of Kupalo. This is the only day of the year I can give you orders, Father. And you must follow them if you want to see the Solstice through. Today is *my* day and you know it."

I turned and saw frightened faces peering out from behind the bend of the stone wall. Praskovia and her maids—Lubava and Nastya, I believe. Pavel, the stable man. Some more people I barely knew.

"Release this man," I said into space. "Take him to the servants' quarters. Dress his wounds. See to his needs. Today he is mine. Tomorrow my father and I will decide his fate."

I felt my father's gaze burn the back of my neck, but I ignored it as I strode through the crowd hastily parting before me, and made my way back upstairs.

IVAN

As the thicket concealing Baba Yaga's lair fell further behind, the walking became easier. Sticky branches no longer grabbed at Ivan's legs in an attempt to slow him down. Hazel leaves didn't try to slap him in the face. Instead, the welcoming shapes of slender birches rose ahead, letting glimpses of sunlight through their airy crowns.

It was unusual for Wolf to trot behind Ivan instead of leading the way. As they walked, Ivan threw quick glances over his shoulder at the gray shape. He itched to ask a question, but he knew better.

As the trees became scarcer, Wolf finally came up by Ivan's side. "You have a question, boy?"

"Yes."

"Then ask. I can stand no more of your fidgeting."

Ivan turned to face the beast. "What did you do to make Baba Yaga so angry with you? Why did she curse you out of your speech?"

There was a pause. For a while Ivan thought he wasn't going to get an answer. Then, for a while longer he thought of worse things that could happen if he went too far with Wolf.

When Wolf finally spoke, his answer came as a dart out of nowhere. Ivan almost jumped at the sound of Wolf's familiar voice.

"There was a girl. Yaga's ward. Her kin."

In the in silence that followed Ivan had time to give up on the rest of the story. Then Wolf spoke again.

"Elena. She was the most beautiful woman in the world."

"And?" Ivan prompted.

165

Wolf growled. "If you're going to interrupt, boy, why don't you do the talking?"

"Sorry. I won't interrupt you again."

They covered a lot of distance before the story continued.

"Yaga never said where Elena came from. The girl might have been her own daughter, for all I know. Or, perhaps Yaga and her sisters brewed the girl up in one of those giant kettles they use for their unspeakable herb stews. Whatever the origin, Yaga couldn't keep the girl with her. The old woman's a loner. There's no room for two in her chicken-legged hut. Besides, the forest thicket is hardly a place for a healthy young girl."

How could they *brew* someone in a kettle? And who were Yaga's sisters? Ivan bit back the questions.

"So," Wolf went on, "she released Elena into my care. She trusted me back then. And I, I took Elena to the only man I could trust to raise her among humans. A herb man, who already had another daughter to make Elena a perfect younger sister."

Realization dawned. "Gleb," Ivan whispered.

"Yes, Gleb. Gleb and his daughter, Praskovia."

Ivan tried to remember everything he knew about Gleb. There wasn't much to recall; the old herb man had spoken a lot, but told nothing about himself, only about Kashchey and Marya. Wolf had called Gleb *his* herb man. He'd spoken of Gleb giving up, so that Wolf had to find another herb man, Nikifor. Another herb man with a sad Solstice story. Perhaps Gleb, like Nikifor, had lost a daughter in a Solstice sacrifice?

The guessing must have shown on Ivan's face.

"Don't think you're that smart, boy. You think you know everything now, but you don't. Elena left Gleb of her own free will. She met a man she loved, and Gleb, as a good father, saw nothing wrong in blessing her marriage."

"Then—" Ivan asked carefully, "what did happen to Elena?"

"Let's just say that whatever happened, Baba Yaga blamed me for her fate."

"You?"

Wolf shook his head. "If I hadn't given Elena to Gleb, if I had interfered when she was leaving Gleb's house to make her own home, if I had intervened at some point before it was too late, I could have saved her. Perhaps. I was right there, you know. But I didn't. So, when the curse Yaga put on me almost turned me into an ordinary beast, I felt I deserved it." He fell silent and trotted ahead.

Ivan didn't dare to ask any more. But after a *versta* or two Wolf spoke again.

"You asked me once, why do I want to bring down Kashchey and see the prophecy come true. I guess now that we're about to fulfill it, you deserve to know the truth. Of course, you'll probably die and I'll blame myself for your death, as well as the deaths of all those others who failed before you. Perhaps Yaga is right. There is no undoing what has been done. But, as far as I reckon, it's well worth it to try to prevent such a thing from happening again."

Ivan stared, his skin tingling with the guess he didn't want to venture. "It was Kashchey who married Elena?"

"No. Kashchey wasn't the one who married her. But he was the one who killed her."

Ivan hadn't realized how familiar the forest had become until they were back in the sickly swamps of the Thirty Ninth Kingdom. Old, gnarled trees hung out their lichen beards, like village matrons hanging sheets out to dry in the sun.

It was late afternoon, but the sun was still high in the sky. Thankfully, it was the longest day of the year and sunset wasn't due for least several hours.

They stopped under a bearded tree.

"Now I must tell you what to do," Wolf said. "Or, more importantly, what *not* to do."

"I think I know what to do," Ivan said. He immediately regretted his words, but it was too late.

"Oh, do you now? I can only imagine."

Ivan thought it best to stand his ground. "We have the

Needle, so Kashchey cannot harm us, right? And Marya—doesn't she have to consent to marry me after I give her the Water?"

"Do you want her to?"

Ivan forced away the warmth that spread through his body at the mere thought of seeing her again. He longed to touch her again, to hold her hand, to look into her eyes. To see—maybe—that look of a trapped animal in her eyes melt away. To hear her laugh, just once?

He couldn't afford such thoughts. Not now.

He shook his head. "Not against her will. I would never force such a thing."

"I suppose you should have thought of that before invoking a sacred ritual by asking for her hand."

"Will she have to?"

"Before the Sacrifice is made, she doesn't *have to* do anything. It's the Solstice. She's the Mistress. She rules the night."

Ivan's expression changed to uncertainty. "But I thought—"

"What?"

"Nothing."

"You thought that she'd fall into your arms the minute she sees you, right? How could she, a powerful sorceress, the most beautiful woman in the world, resist such a charmer as you?"

Ivan raised his head and looked into the distance with unfocused eyes. "You're right, of course. But ritual or not, I will never marry her against her will. She deserves a choice. She deserves a *life*, like any other young girl. She deserves a man she would love with all her heart. I'd rather die than force her."

Wolf looked at him sideways. "It would seem that you have plenty of opportunities to die without inventing more. Why don't we talk of important things instead, shall we?"

Ivan turned his head. There was a new expression in his eyes, their cornflower blue shaded by an overcast sky. "Of course. We should talk about important things instead."

"Just after the girl disappears under the water, step forward

168

and make your claim."

"Right."

"*After* the sacrifice is over—not before. And, no foolish deeds. No jumping into the water to rescue the girl, do you hear? It's deadly in there. Vodyanoy himself is at work, and he never lets anyone slip his grasp."

"But—we can't just let the girl die," Ivan protested. "If I came in right before the Sacrifice—"

"Then Marya will do whatever she wants with you. On the night of the Solstice, she is all-powerful. After the Sacrifice is done, the power goes to her father. Yet, while he is devouring the girl's soul, he's vulnerable. That's when we make our move."

"We can't just stand there and let the girl drown."

"We can. We must, if you truly want to put a stop to it. Don't even think of jumping into the water, Ivan the Fool. You'll have your chance to die if you miss the right moment with Kashchey. Or, with your lovely bride to be. Do you understand?"

"Yes." Ivan sighed.

"Good. Now, remember: you talk to Marya and I'll handle Kashchey. Promise me you won't try to interfere."

"I promise."

Wolf nodded. "Remember, boy, No one has ever come this close. No one, in all the history of this kingdom. It's all up to you. Don't ruin it."

"I won't."

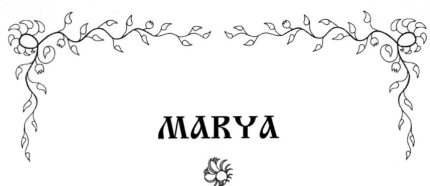

MARYA

The surface of the lake was still as a mirror, reflecting the blue and pink of the sunset sky. The evening mist floated over the water, its flat wisps spreading through the tall reeds whose thickets treacherously concealed the real banks of the lake. Tiny swirls of current circled under the smooth surface. I knew the lake like a horse knows its stead. I knew exactly where to come to the shore, through the invisible paths among the reeds. I knew where one could enter the water safely, and where the treacherous current pulled you right down, into the weeds that would hold you underwater to your death.

The air was still and sweet-smelling. Even the birds were silent in that sacred hour when the Mistress of the Solstice took her lonely bath in the clear waters of the lake. I had to be clean like a newborn child when I went to collect the twelve secret herbs for the Drink of Love that would then be distributed to everyone attending the ritual. My servants in the glade were already starting the fire and boiling the water in a huge kettle, getting everything ready for me to do my part.

The water felt warm, like milk fresh from a cow. I felt the currents caressing my body, gently pulling me into their flow. I floated easily in their supporting hands, admiring the smooth spears of the reeds going down through the dark amber water, clear all the way to the bottom where green weeds waved like long strands of hair. Further upstream was a wide, deep place where the turmoil of the water created a standing whirlpool. The Sacrifice Pool. Treacherously calm on the surface, the waters in that place pulled you right in to the wavering locks of green slimy weeds on the bottom, weeds that caught you in their net of death. That was the place where the maiden was sacrificed. Where Alyona would disappear today, as many girls had before her.

I tried to relax and enjoy my swim. I turned onto my back in the slow wide stream, letting the lake carry me, letting my hair lie loose on the surface, wavering in the current just like the green weeds wavered along the bottom in the amber depths beneath me. My body took on a faintly yellow tint where the amber waters covered it. I watched the clear sky above gradually change from light blue and pink to deeper blue and crimson, before finally acquiring the sapphire tones of the early evening.

A lonely star shimmered just above the horizon. The air outside started feeling cooler than the water. Time to go.

With slight movements of my arms I used the current to take me to the shore, where my servants waited with my ritual dress. Unlike my usual black garment, this dress was white, and the wreath that covered my head, unlike any other flower-wreath of tonight, was made of white water-lilies, the kind that usually faded almost immediately after you picked them, but that always stayed fresh when they crowned my hair on the night of the Solstice.

I stood still while the servants dried my body and hair with a long soft cloth and clad me in my ritual outfit. The only words I could say before the Drink of Love was ready were the words of the enchanted rhyme of the twelve herbs, and I could only even say the rhyme to myself. Nobody else in the whole kingdom knew that rhyme, an ancient incantation that could only be passed from one Mistress of the Solstice to another.

When my servants were done, I passed dreamily out of their hands to wander the forest in search of the twelve herbs.

I enjoyed that quiet evening hour all by myself in the slumbering forest, where no sounds could be heard. I walked among the trees, through the glades, along the riverbanks. I sought out the twelve sacred herbs, collecting them, counting them by the slow rhythm of the incantation.

Thick, fleshy catnip stems crowned by their umbrella-like inflorescence of tiny blossoms.

Cozy, yellow-and-white chamomiles with their bitter medicinal smell.

Elegant lychnis with its small flowers of fluffy pink, resembling tiny campfires—the villagers actually called it *goritsvet*, fire-flower.

I collected the sweet plump balls of heady wild clover, and the long and fragile stems of pretty bluebells. From open glades I walked closer to the water to seek out the tall rose-bay plants with their pink, brush-like tips covered with flowers. Rose-bay added substance to the brew. Villagers called it "tea-plant", and it was the one that gave the potion its special tartness, fragrant with the herbs and rich with the magic of Kupalo.

All the time I was reciting to myself:

> *Herbs of the magic brew, six and six,*
> *Blend at my will into potent mix.*
> *Six herbs of darkness, six herbs of light,*
> *Grant me the power, grant me the sight.*

> *Light herbs are easy—pick them and toss them:*
> *Color of bluebell, chamomile blossom,*
> *Freshness of catnip, honey of clover,*
> *Fire of lychnis, rose-bay flower.*

It was now time to pick the six herbs of the dark, so I changed my rhyme:

> *Herbs of the dark are heady and strong,*
> *Pick them is silence, sing them no song.*
> *Dark herbs that seal the brew's potent taste*
> *Cannot be named, or your work is a waste.*

I moved to the drier places, away from the water, where

the fir trees clumped together guarding the darker part of the woods. Inhaling deeply the fresh smells of fir and earth, I tossed my damp hair behind my back and bent closer to the grass, trying to spot the deep purple flowers of nightshade. I only needed a few, and this was the perfect spot to find them.

A glimpse of purple caught my eye. I stuck my free hand into the tall grass and pulled out a flower.

Panic-stricken, I held it before my eyes. The pile of freshly collected herbs poured down from my arms like a rain of smells and colors. I froze with terror, looking at the flower in my hand.

Purple leaves on top almost hid from my eye the delicate yellow flowers underneath.

Ivan-and-Marya.

I never needed that plant in my brew. As far as I knew, it had never grown in that spot before, in the deep grass under the low fir branches. What kind of strange power had made me stumble upon it now, at this sacred moment? What power drove me not only to notice it in the grass, but to mistakenly pick it up?

I threw the purple-and-yellow flower as far away as I could. I sank down into the grass to collect the sacred herbs I'd dropped, and to regain the concentration I needed to finish my task.

When I finally entered the glade where the Solstice celebration was to take place, it was almost dark. One could still see some light crowning the tops of the trees surrounding the glade from the west, but it would soon fade, dimmed by the giant bonfire in the center of the open space. I walked slowly, straight to the fire, where a huge boiling kettle was set aside for me to make my brew. I walked, barely noticing the people circling the glade, people wearing wreaths of wild flowers around their heads, people hastily moving aside to make way for me. I walked, my arms full of herbs, the incantation with its slow rhythm sounding in my head.

Praskovia stepped forward and led me through, into the circle formed by my serving women around the kettle. They hid me from view, providing a lonely spot in the midst of chaos for me to do my magic. I settled on the grass, chanting, sorting out the herbs, counting their stems to make the exact amount needed for the Drink of Love.

Herbs of the magic brew, six and six,
Blend at my will into potent mix.

I counted bluebells, crushing them with my hands as I threw them into the pot, one by one. The water, could I have seen it clearly in that light, turned a light pink. I added chamomile flowers, snipping them off their long leathery stems. Chamomile added a strong flavor, and the boiling gave off a tart smell. My head cleared as I submerged myself into the realm of heady fumes emanating from the kettle. This was my world. I felt strong in it.

Six herbs of darkness, six herbs of light,
Grant me the power, grant me the sight.

Through the air of detachment surrounding me I could hear the voices outside my magic circle, people singing as they circled in a dance around the glade, but I paid no heed to them.

Light herbs are easy—pick them and toss them:
Color of bluebell, chamomile blossom,
Freshness of catnip, honey of clover,
Fire of lychnis, rose-bay flower.

Catnip plants sank into the thickening depths of the kettle, followed by fragrant heads of honeyed clover, bright spots of lychnis, and armfuls of rose-bay. My pile of herbs was getting small as the brew became fuller, gradually acquiring the rich, sweet smell that would make my head swim if I inhaled it too deeply.

But the brew was only half-finished, and the smell had not

yet acquired its special heady touch.

I watched the brew grow dark, swirling as the last of the rose-bay blossoms disappeared into its dark depths. And then the color of the brew began to fade, so that in the wavering light of the bonfire, it looked almost the color of light amethyst. Amethyst, the stone of soberness.

It was time for the dark ingredients, only a few of them, but necessary for that special final touch, signaled by the heady smell that made one feel lightheaded when the drink came into its full, magic power.

To do this right, I had to be detached, concentrating fully on the task at hand, and yet, secretly, at this time of all others, I was most vulnerable to the influence of emotions.

> *Dark herbs that seal the brew's potent taste*
> *Cannot be named, or your work is a waste.*

I felt a little disoriented as I threw in the last ingredient and spoke in my head the last line of the incantation.

The Drink of Love was ready.

Alyona was beautiful in her ceremonial garb that mirrored mine—a long white dress, a wreath of lilies crowning her long, loose hair. She looked ghostly, almost transparent, as she was led through the glade by a procession of men and women from the palace, each holding a candle in their hands. My kiss shone on her forehead like a five-pointed star. Her eyes were closed and my father, walking behind, carefully guided her steps, extending his calming magic to keep her in check.

A fine gift to the Solstice. Just like the ones that came before, just like the ones who would come after, for ages to be.

As the procession stopped before me, I swallowed a mouthful of the rich, bittersweet brew and, fighting to suppress the feeling of lightheadedness it gave me, held out the ladle for Alyona to drink. My father and two serving women had to guide her to me and support her as she took a sip with trembling lips.

At least, she isn't crying anymore, I thought. *I hope she holds together until the end.*

As she swallowed the bittersweet drink, she trembled from head to toe, and, with a small shudder, moved on like a sleepwalker, guided by the women's hands.

I served the drink to my father, briefly meeting his dark impenetrable gaze, and continued to hold out the ladle for each and every one of my subjects, trying to distance myself from the power of the brew until the giant kettle was almost empty, and there were no more people waiting to receive their share.

By now everyone crowded at the edge of the Sacrifice Pool, carrying tiny candles they would later put into their flower-wreaths before they sent them floating on the waters of the lake. It was the Solstice way of fortune-telling. If a wreath floated for a long time, its owner's fortune was good. If it sank straight to the bottom, it meant death. Tiny dots of candles reflected in the dark, still waters of the lake like stars, flickering in the slight movement of the night air.

Two women at Alyona's sides pulled off her white dress, leaving her naked. She was to be given to Kupalo as a bride, and her white garments had to fall for their wedding night. I admired her beauty in the wavering candlelight. She may have been imperfect as a common village girl, but the aura of the Solstice made her look like an immortal spirit of the river. Everyone stepped aside as I approached her and laid my hands on her shoulders. Then I spoke, for the first time since the beginning of the evening.

"Great God Kupalo," I said. "Accept this maiden as our gift to your powers and a token of the coming season. May love stay with your subjects, may our fields be fertile and our cattle be aplenty, may you take what you need and leave us what you will."

I kissed her on the forehead again, and this time the star faded; she opened her eyes as if awakening, and looked at me with terror, shivering from head to foot.

"Go," I whispered to her, turning her around and pushing her gently toward the water.

Her legs trembled, but she managed to take those few necessary steps forward before they gave way. Luckily, it was enough. With the last step she sank into the whirlpool.

She disappeared from sight almost instantly, without struggle. As the water covered the top of her head, her lily wreath came loose, floated a little way, then sank beside her.

I let out a barely perceptible sigh. It was done. Another season. Another Solstice.

I shut my eyes as I sensed my father step up beside me.

"Marya," he whispered. "Well done. Now, bring her to me."

I felt his shiver, sensed his anticipation as it echoed through me. I stretched out my thoughts, searching—

—a movement in the bushes invaded on my concentration, approaching, morphing into loud cracking as somebody pushed his way through the thicket to the shore by the Sacrifice Pool.

I opened my eyes.

The boy, Ivan, stood in front of me. His shirt was torn at the shoulder and bits of branches stuck out of his hair. And, he was smiling with that foolish smile of his. I felt a rush of warmth as I met his gaze and resisted an urge to smile back as I lowered my eyes to his outstretched hand.

He held—

A vial of glowing liquid.

"I'm back, Marya," he said. "I fulfilled your task. I brought it to you."

I opened my mouth, but no words came.

It simply couldn't be.

Not *now*.

"What is this?" I demanded.

Ivan's smiled widened. He looked like a proud child bringing his mama a prize.

"Water of Life," he said. "From the Hidden Stream. Just like you asked. And, it is still Solstice night. So, I have fulfilled your task, beautiful Marya. And now—"

"This can't be," I whispered. "I don't believe you. You *couldn't* have done it. I gave you a task impossible to fulfill."

My father stepped between us. "Begone, boy! we'll deal with you later."

Ivan's gaze hardened. "You haven't devoured the virgin soul yet, Kashchey, And I won't let you. Not this time."

"Oh, yes? And you can stop me?"

A low growl came from the darkness, and my father froze. A great shape stepped from behind Ivan.

"I can," Wolf said.

He looked exactly like a wolf, but his head came up almost to Ivan's shoulder. A giant wolf. A beast of great magic. I suddenly realized that the space around us was empty. With the Sacrifice over, all the people had already returned to the glade and the bonfire to partake in the food and merrymaking. It was just the four of us by the water. Me and my father. Ivan and the Gray Wolf.

"I will stop you, Kashchey," Wolf said. "Now, boy—"

But Ivan wasn't listening. He stood by the edge of the water, a glowing vial in his hand.

"I can bring her back," he said, his voice almost a whisper. "She—she doesn't deserve to die. Not like this."

"Don't you dare," Wolf warned him.

Ivan raised his eyes and looked at all of us. His gaze softened as it slid over me, and I felt a warmth flow through me again, as if I was touched by a passing beam of sun. Then, he pulled off his shirt and I finally saw it live. A birthmark shaped exactly like an arrow. It marked his left shoulder, tilted to point more of less straight at his heart, and in the light of the candles now floating on the lake in their boats of flower wreaths, it glistened almost like gold.

On the night of the Solstice, a hero of legend cometh marked by an arrow through turmoil and gloom. How could I remember these words so well when I only heard them once?

"Forgive me," Ivan said. "But I can't do it any other way."

He jumped into the Sacrifice Pool and disappeared underwater.

I felt the air swish around me, as if the forest itself exhaled a breath it was holding. My heart quivered as I looked at the water that rippled briefly and closed over his head. So quickly.

"Good," my father said. "He saved us the trouble."

Wolf's muttered curse made the grass around his feet wither and turn yellow.

I stepped closer to the water, my eyes straining to make out shapes in the turmoil under its dark surface.

I could see no movement down there.

There was no escape from the Sacrifice Pool.

IVAN

Ivan was a good swimmer, yet no skill, no strength could possibly work against the deadly pull he felt. The waters grabbed his body like a rag and drew him down, down, straight to the weeds on the bottom.

His vision faded as he descended, but he could still see another body tangled in the weeds down there. A naked woman.

Dead.

"Alyona—" he whispered mutely, moving his lips against the sandy thickness of the cold water. It was getting darker. The fingers of the current tangled the weeds around his struggling legs. His arm brushed the skin of Alyona's lifeless hand and sank into the silky green of the weed thicket.

His lungs were burning. Soon, he would have to take a breath.

One—last—breath—

It was useless to fight. He could no longer tell if it was getting darker because of the deepening night or because his eyes refused to serve him anymore. He forced his eyes to stay open, straining to see light up above, at the lake's surface.

Marya—
Wolf—
I have—failed—you—
There is no—forgiveness—for what I have done—
I didn't listen—
I failed—
Forgive me. Forgive me if you can.

He opened his mouth to take a breath.

And closed it again.

180

A hollow string of a reed descended from the surface. It forced itself through his clenched teeth. Then, a voice he didn't recognize whispered into his ear.

"Blow out the water. Then, breathe through the reed."

He grasped it.

Blow out—

Breathe—

Air rushed to his burning lungs.

Air.

"Breathe," the voice said. "Breathe, Ivan the Fool."

He did. For a while all he could focus on was the flow of air—so painfully slow through the thin reed—into his hungry lungs. He gathered a whole chestful of it and held it in until he felt he would burst. Then, he let it out, watching the bubbles rise in silvery trails up to the surface.

For a while his life narrowed to just breathing—breathe in, breathe out. At first, he gave no thought to the voice he'd heard so effortlessly as if they two were standing in the middle of a forest glade. Then, as his breathing became almost normal, he began to wonder.

He tried to turn his head, but his body was now so tangled in the weeds he couldn't move.

He tried to speak. Words came out as a gurgle, filling his mouth with muddy water.

"Who are you?"

He heard laughter. A girlish giggle.

"Don't try to speak. Just think. Underwater, your thoughts are loud as bells. I'm not deaf."

Who are you? he thought.

"You don't remember me? I'm Oksana, the Wandering Light, remember? You gave me my nickname less than a fortnight ago. Do you remember?"

Oksana. The kikimora from Leshy's swamp.

Of course he remembered. Even without the uncanny laughter, he would never be able to forget the undead child with glowing tree rot in her hands. Her eyes—he would never forget her eyes.

How did you find me?

She giggled again. "I'm glad you remember me, Ivan the Fool. It's so sweet of you to think you could never forget me! I will always remember you too. That's why I followed you when I saw you making your way here. These waters connect to our swamp, you know. When the bodies rot here and the pieces start falling off, some of them come to us in the swamp and our animals—they all have such a feast! I wish I could enjoy rotten meat as much as they do! But I don't eat those things anymore..." She chattered away, just like a lonely child who finally found a playmate. "The animals would like to come here and get the rotting meat, but they shouldn't, you know. The swamp—that's Uncle Leshy's place, but here on the lake, it all belongs to Uncle Vodyanoy. You know him of course, don't you?"

The Water Man. I know of him, he thought wearily. *If Leshy plays riddles that one can sometimes win, Vodyanoy plays in drowning people. One can never win that game.*

She stopped chattering to listen to his thoughts and then floated into view from behind him—a little girl in a loose white dress. She still held her glowing piece of wood, unnaturally bright in the dimness at the bottom of the lake. Ivan briefly wondered how could wood continue to glow underwater, but it didn't really matter. Not in his sorry state, with Oksana his savior and his only company. He focused on watching her hair instead, falling in waves over her shoulders—as if she wasn't underwater but was standing in the middle of her little island amidst the swamp.

"That's where you're wrong, Ivan the Fool," she said solemnly. "Uncle Vodyanoy is very kind. He plays with me. He brings me toys sometimes. Uncle Leshy never does."

Of course, he thought. *My mistake. Sorry.*

"You haven't heard the best part yet." She leaned in to Ivan so that their noses almost touched, her eyes shining with mischief. "He said, because I'm such a good playmate, and you're my friend, he's going to let you go. And, if you want, you can take *her* as well." She nodded at Alyona's body, tangled in the weeds beside him. "That's why you're here, aren't you? Even though the animals in the swamp will be very disappointed. No rotten meat this time."

Vodyanoy would do that? Really?

"Yes!" she giggled again. "I told you he's real nice!"

Yes, he is, Ivan though wholeheartedly. *Only, even if he lets me go, there's no way I can untangle myself from these weeds.*

"Not by yourself," she agreed. "The *rusalkas* will help you."

Rusalkas?

He felt cold fingers pull at the weeds around his legs and turned to see pale shapes moving in the murky waters. Now they looked like women and then, when they turned, they looked more like giant scaly pike. *Rusalkas.* He'd heard about them. Leshy and Vodyanoy, the two brothers, spawned many curious creatures.

They untangled Alyona's body while he watched, and then the underwater current caught it, flipped it over, and gently dragged it along the bottom.

"You can swim, can't you?" Oksana asked.

Yes, I can, he thought. *If the weeds don't hold me again.*

"They won't," she promised. "Just swim downstream and come out on shore over there. You can take her." She nodded at Alyona's body, disappearing into the darkness as the currents became bolder with it.

I don't know how to thank you Oksana, he thought. *I –*

"You already did," she said. "You gave me my nickname. It's been all right ever since. I'm not Oksana With No Nickname anymore. And uncle Leshy doesn't tease me anymore. Now, they all know who I am!"

I'll bring some meat for your swamp creatures, he promised. *A whole cow, if you want.*

"No," she twitched her nose. "They could never eat a *cow.* But you can throw in some rabbits over there. Skinned. They'd like that."

She turned and moved away in the water. Or, she didn't exactly move, but suddenly she was standing several paces away. Her outline began to fade.

Thank you, Oksana!

"Think nothing of it, Ivan the Fool! Until next time!"

And then she was gone.

He clenched the lifesaving reed between his teeth and swam ahead to catch up with Alyona's body. It had caught on a boulder and was lying still, curved around the rough stone surface. He turned it over and hauled it onto his back. The body was limp and it caught on reeds and underwater boulders as he hauled it along. But, if nothing else interfered, he would be able to take it up to the shore, just visible in the gloom ahead.

He grasped a dead arm firmly and kicked toward the shore.

MARYA

The silence grew heavy between us. Raven flew out of the darkness and landed on a nearby branch.

He never came around for the Solstice Sacrifice. He looked so out of place in the moonlit glade by the water. Even though I knew of his nightly forays to this spot, he belonged on his perch in my room, a comfortable companion in my lonely hours.

He briefly glanced at the dark waters of the pool and looked away as he settled on the protruding branch. "I couldn't miss the prophecy coming true."

"You just did," my father said. "The boy sacrificed himself to Kupalo."

I looked at Wolf, a knot of grayness against the dark forest. He faded into the background as his yellow eyes shut for an endless moment, but then they opened again, and more grass withered under his feet.

Then, he pricked his years and stood up, his Primal senses catching something that eluded the rest of us.

In a few moments we all heard it.

Distant splashing, a rustling of reeds around the bend of the lake, a faint sound that became louder as something—somebody–came crushing toward us through the forest undergrowth.

A silhouette took shape, visible through the reed-choked shoreline against the flashes of the bonfire. A man carrying something heavy in his arms. A body... *A naked woman.*

"Alyona." My eyes welled with tears as I watched Ivan lay her gently on the ground at our feet.

She looked quite dead. Splotches of green weeds covered

her arms and legs and tangled in her long wet hair. She was paler than the moon now shining brightly in the sky, and her half-opened eyes held no spark of life in them. Her skin was torn where her body must have brushed against underwater rocks, and a grimace of agony bared her teeth, twisting her once pretty face into an ugly snarl.

I felt nausea rise, as if somebody had punched me in the stomach. My legs folded under me and I sank to the ground by Alyona's side. Tears prickled at the back of my throat. I swallowed them, forced them down as I took her cold stiff hands, clenched together in what must have been an attempt to free herself from the deadly weeds.

Never before had I been forced to see the result of my deeds. And now, there was no way to deny this anymore. I killed her. I had killed many others before her.

What have I done?

Tears rolled down my cheeks, and I made no move to hold them back anymore.

"Don't worry, Marya," Ivan said gently. "She will be all right."

Once again, he pulled out the glowing vial from his belt. Mesmerized, I watched him open the lid and sprinkle water over Alyona's body.

As soon as the droplets touched her face, her grimace smoothed into a peaceful expression. Color flowed back into her cheeks. Her eyes closed and then reopened, filled with new life.

"Mistress," she whispered.

I wanted to speak, to reassure her that it was all over, but the treacherous tears were back in my throat. I held the tears back. My voice stayed with them. All I could do was shake my head, clenching her now-warm hand in both of mine.

I had never seen the Water of Life do its work before.

The words of the prophecy rang in my head. *He bringeth new life for the new sacrifice.*

I looked at Ivan in wonder. *How did he do it?*

And then another, horrifying thought came, unbidden.

What will happen to my father now, without a soul to feed him?

"Get up, girl," the Gray Wolf said to Alyona. "It's over. Nobody is going to hurt you again."

"Here is your dress," Ivan said, reappearing from somewhere with her ceremonial dress in his hands.

We helped her back into the dress and I smoothed her hair, still unable to speak. Then Praskovia and her maids stepped out of the forest from the direction of the bonfire glade and silently led Alyona away.

"Now," my father said to Ivan. "Give me back the Needle."

The Gray Wolf stepped forward to Ivan's side. "I've volunteered to be its keeper, Kashchey. We have some business to finish." He smacked his lips and I saw the glistening Needle sticking out of his mouth, between his teeth, just as if he were chewing a glistening stem of grass.

I saw my father go pale.

"Give it to me!" he demanded.

"Come, Kashchey. Let's settle some scores, shall we? You owe it to Marya."

To me? What kind of nonsense was this? I was the one who owed everything to my father. My powers, my high station, my life. What could Wolf possibly mean?

"Leave Marya out of this." A falter in Father's voice made me shiver. Was he *afraid*?

He didn't devour the virgin's soul. Of, Gods, I failed him, all because of my foolishness.

Wolf took another step toward my father. "You owe her this, Kashchey. She always thought you were her closest kin. Have the courage to tell her yourself. Whose daughter is she?"

"Mine!"

Wolf bit gently on the Needle in his mouth and my father's face twitched. In pain? Anger? I couldn't tell.

"Let it be, Wolf," Raven said quietly. I turned to him in surprise. Such pain in his voice.

Stop! I wanted to shout. *Stop hurting my father and Raven, the two wise, powerful beings who made up my whole world. Stop causing them pain.* And more than that, I realized. I did not

187

want to learn why this conversation pained them. If I did, my whole world would fall apart. I knew this much.

But I had no power to stop it.

"All right!" Father said. "So, Marya is Raven's daughter. What difference does it make?"

What? The world around me was going mad. *Me? Raven's daughter?*

"He gave her up of his own free will!" my father said.

Wolf shook his head. "His spirit was broken, Kashchey, and you took advantage, because she was so perfect for you."

Enough. Stop this madness at once. "What are you all talking about?" I demanded.

Wolf turned his gray snout to me.

His eyes shone like two yellow moons, moons marred with vertical slits of deeper orange. His gaze drew me in. Two pools of light filled my vision, momentarily blinding me with their brightness. Then the light faded to normal, and I stood looking at a forest meadow, and a cozy little house cradled in the curve of a quietly tinkling brook.

I've seen this place before. Where?

In my dreams, perhaps?

A young woman ran into sight. She was laughing. A wreath of wild asters crowned her head and she carried a bunch of forest bluebells. She sank onto the grass by the brook and dropped the flowers, breathing heavily and looking with expectation back in the direction from whence she'd come.

She was so beautiful that my breath caught with longing. I watched the perfect movements of her slender fingers stroke the flower stems, then smooth the waves of her long black hair. I admired the elegant line of her neck, and her clear green eyes, glowing like two emeralds in her warm, lively face. They were filled with laughter, and like her whole being, emanated happiness and health.

She could have been the image of me, had she not been so warm, so happy, so full of life and love. No one would ever mistake her for me.

Who is she?

The girl didn't have long to wait. Another shape emerged from behind the bushes at the edge of the glade. A man. Pale, dark-haired, with dreamy eyes and a beaked nose.

He sat on the grass next to her. They looked into each other's eyes and laughed. Then she fell into his arms and, after a lifetime of embraces and kisses, settled with her head on his lap. She was like a cat, playing with her bluebells, quite content with herself. The man looked down at her with such happiness that my heart ached for him.

Distantly I could hear faint sounds from the world I'd left behind when I submerged into the yellow depths of Wolf's eyes, but they meant nothing in the face of this strangely familiar scene.

It was like looking into my Mirror, but infinitely more real. I could even smell the flowers in her hands, the fragrance of her skin, fresh like water in a clear forest spring.

The love in the man's eyes was unbearable to watch.

"I have to go, Elena." His voice was low, and deeper than I would have expected from his slight frame. And it was so familiar that I could almost sense his presence, somewhere, just out of my reach.

"Will you be long?" she asked, much too busy weaving together a garland of bluebell stems to return the man's look.

Such anguish in his eyes! Such pain at leaving her!

Why am I forced to watch this?

I struggled to break free, but couldn't. Wolf held me firmly in his power.

"No, my love," his voice was almost a whisper. "I'll be back soon."

She lifted her head as he stood, but she didn't get up with him. She lay sprawled on the grass, watching him like a playful kitten.

The man shifted shape.

It was fascinating to watch. I must look like this when I change into a dove, but I'd never watched myself do it. He bent and his form shrank into a small black shape. Where a man had stood a moment ago, there was now a bird.

189

Raven?

He spread his wings and flew out of sight.

I drew away from Wolf, breathing hard. Everyone watched me intently. But I had eyes only for the black bird, motionless on his branch.

"Raven?" I gasped.

"What did the beast show you?" my father demanded.

For the first time in my life I ignored him. I couldn't take my eyes off Raven's still form.

"You had a human form?" I whispered.

He shut his eyes.

Wolf nudged me. "That's not the end of the story. Watch closely, Marya."

"What is this?" I demanded. "What kind of magic are you imposing on me?"

"The same magic as is contained within your Mirror. The magic of the Primals. Now, watch, girl, before I lose my patience."

I didn't want to watch. But I couldn't help it.

The maiden, Elena, was now alone. She left her bluebells heaped on the grass and walked into the house. A moment later she came out again to look up into the sky.

And then a new figure appeared in the glade.

My heart leapt, then stood still in my chest.

He walked with the confident, springing steps of a born charmer, a conqueror who had just spotted prey worthy of his attention.

My father, Kashchey the Immortal.

I'd been told that, in the old days, he'd used charm to win his women rather than brutal force. Even in my day I had seen it often enough to recognize that seductive look on his face. Worse, I saw a matching look of interest in the girl's green eyes, imperfectly concealed by a charming expression of boredom.

I didn't need to watch further to know what happened next.

"Enough," I said, stepping away from Wolf. "I don't want to watch any more. I don't see why you have to show me this."

My father's victories over women often had unfair and destructive consequences, but I'd learned long ago not to care.
Now, here, in my unbalanced state, I didn't want another desperate story forced on me. So, my father had taken away
Raven's love. That was between the two of them. Why did I
have to care?

Wolf's rumbling growl vibrated through the ground.

"Step away from him, Marya!" my father ordered. "You
don't have to submit to this nonsense!"

"Oh, yes, she does." Wolf smiled through clenched teeth.
He looked into my eyes again with his shining yellow gaze
and I couldn't resist him anymore.

It was as I'd expected. The airy-headed maiden fell head
over heels in love with my charming father and followed
him to his castle. In her short farewell, she told Raven that
Kashchey was her true love, and the silly bird-man gave her
his blessing instead of beating some sense into her foolish
head.

His grief was hard to watch. He shook with it for what
seemed like weeks. Months? I could not tell. When he had
finally composed himself, he walked out of his little cottage
and, under a dawn sky, he turned himself into Raven again.
And then, he had spoken the words whose power shook the
glade, the forest, and the cottage.

I didn't understand them, but as a shape-shifter, I knew.
He had forsaken his human form. He had locked himself into
his bird form for eternity.

This was why I had never known he had been a human
once.

But there was still more to see.

The vision shifted to our city, to the plaza in front of the
castle that I instantly recognized. Elena emerged from the
main gate and walked up to two people waiting for her on
the cobblestones. The first, a tall thin girl with a long braid,
looked familiar. The way she moved, the majestic posture that
made her look like a noblewoman despite her simple peasant
dress. She turned and I saw the familiar curve of her neck,

the line of her round cheek, sweet and glowing like a young peach.

Praskovia?

I knew she'd been a beauty in the past, but I'd never realized the majesty of her noble grace. It made here stand out even next to Elena, surely the most beautiful woman in the world.

A movement in the tall narrow window above their heads caught my attention. My father's face came into view. He also spotted Praskovia. The predator's glint in his eyes had returned. But his look quickly faded to boredom as he slid his eyes over Elena. Neither of the girls noticed him.

I recognized the man standing next to them. He was younger, and his beard and long straight hair weren't white, but his light blue eyes shone with that same spirit I'd seen earlier today in my father's dungeon. The man I saved from my father's wrath, now lying upstairs in the castle, safe in my servants' care.

Praskovia's father.

The scene changed, and with a sinking heart I looked into a clearing at the side of the lake, the very same one in which we now stood. I looked down into the mirror gleam of the Sacrifice Pool with its treacherous currents rippling underneath the smooth surface. I looked up, and saw my father and Elena walk out from between the trees and stop to admire the view.

My skin crept as I recognized this scene.

My dream.

Except that now I was an observer, not a participant as I watched Elena walk next to my father in springy, vigorous steps. Blessed Kupalo, what was my bond to this woman?

My heart ached to break free, but I couldn't move. Even if Wolf released me now, I wouldn't be able to stop watching.

I could sense everything through a double pair of eyes. Watching from both aside and within, I felt the touch of the gentle summer breeze, the silky grass at my feet, the pleasant coolness emanating from the water. I sensed the love she felt for the man walking next to her, the man who thought of her with nothing but boredom, whose eyes were already set on his next innocent victim.

I loved and hated him at the same time. And I could not draw my eyes away.

Elena cradled something in her hands. My hand itched as the familiar shape of a warm oval object that seemed to fill it. I felt it so often in my dreams. Except that, unlike me, Elena didn't seem to be bothered by it.

Perhaps because she knew what it was?

"This is a good place to swim," my father said. "The best one on the whole lake."

Don't listen to him! I prayed silently. I didn't care what my father did to his women once he was tired of them, but I didn't want to see it.

I couldn't look away.

"I would love to go for a swim," she said, her face glowing with happiness. She loved him so much. I hated her for that. "But I cannot leave my baby," Elena continued. "She will freeze."

"Give her to me," my father said. "I will keep her warm for you. For us." He gave her an affectionate look that I knew was a lie.

Elena hesitated for a moment. Then she opened her palm and handed the thing she held to my father.

It was an egg. A spotted bird's egg.

"I wish she could grow up to be human," Elena whispered, looking fondly at the egg.

"She will," my father said. "After all, her father had a human form once. After she hatches, I'll teach her to change shape like he used to. Now, go, swim, my love, we'll both be waiting for you right here."

Elena was as silly as I'd suspected. Without hesitation she pulled off her dress and jumped into the Sacrifice Pool. As soon as she did, my father turned and walked back into the forest.

It took her a long time to die.

She struggled against the current that pulled her underwater, against the tugging weed, with more force than I had imagined existed in her slender body. She rose to the surface and the air filled with her pleas and screams. She screamed to my father's retreating back. And then, when she realized fully what he had done, she turned away from him. Her eyes went empty at this realization, but she did not cease her struggle.

I admired her for that.

Not long after her first screams echoed though the woods, a black bird flew out of the trees and darted over the Sacrifice Pool. He must have been nearby, but not close enough at first to see what happened.

Raven circled low over the water, trying to pull her up with his claws, trying to fetch something big enough for her to hold on to. He got so dangerously close that her gripping hands almost pulled him underwater with her.

He would have given his life for her. But in his bird form he could do nothing to help her. If only he hadn't forsaken his human form!

His eyes were two pits of despair as he struggled, drenched and exhausted, unwilling to give up and yet powerless to do anything for his love except to die with her.

In the end he chose life.

Perhaps it was for the sake of the egg, his unborn child, now safely in Kashchey's possession.

As her struggle finally ceased, as the water closed over her head one last time, he dropped in fatigue on the bank of the lake and lay there for a long time.

I had never known before that birds could cry.

I sensed the bonds of Wolf's hold weaken. Numb, I sank onto the grass.

"What did you do to her?" my father demanded.

"I showed her the true story of her birth. From an egg that you hatched, Kashchey."

"What of it?" my father asked. "There is no harm in her knowing that! She was born as a dove, but I taught her to take her human form. Just like I promised her mother."

"And what about Raven?"

"He knew. He didn't seem to care. So I kept her to myself. I brought her up as my own daughter. What else should I have done?"

Wolf fixed him with a long stare, but didn't say anything. Instead he turned to me.

"What you saw, Marya, was more than the story of your birth. It was also the story of the first Solstice Sacrifice in your kingdom. Kashchey devoured her soul, and her love gave him power and eternal youth. It changed him. That's when he realized the tradition must continue, and that the Solstice night—the shortest night of the year—was ideal for this deed."

"Not true," Kashchey protested. "The Solstice tradition and the Kupalo cult go back into the ages."

"Not in this form. Solstice fertility rites are indeed ancient, but they have long become no more than festivities, with some suggestive symbolism. Devouring a virgin's soul to feed your power—that, I can tell you, was your invention, Kashchey."

"But why—?" My lips did not obey me. They felt dry, cracked. Cold. I subsided, listening to Wolf's steady voice.

"Kashchey raised you as his own. He learned to control you with magic, taught you to believe that Solstice Sacrifice in your kingdom was an old and important tradition—all because you were so perfect for this role. You see, for the sacrifice to work, the one conducting it must be untouched by love. He soon found he couldn't do it himself, because his constant love affairs drove him in random and dangerous directions. But if he had a high priestess who could control her feelings so well, he wouldn't have to worry at all."

Control my feelings. I remembered how my father taught me not to form any attachments since early on. How anyone that caught my fancy tended to disappear, until, at thirteen, he had taught me the horrible lesson of lust and love once and for all. I always thought this control was part of my power.

"Before you came of age, he was forced to choose the Mistress of the Solstice from old, spiteful women who had already wasted all their capacity to love in this world. But such women never had enough feelings left inside them to gain him real power. And yet he couldn't use a young woman instead. The Drink of Love, another important component of the rite, is a powerful potion and no young woman could withstand it. You were his perfect chance."

"I don't understand," I whispered.

"You have bird's blood in you. You have much passion, but for the passion you have, you are much more resistant to the urges of human flesh. Only Kashchey, having brought you up, knew how to control you."

Kashchey, so often caressing me; the lovers he'd procured for me. How I'd always longed for his touch more than anything, and yet, we had never taken that longing further than dreams and desire.

It had worked, perfectly. I could never love my father the way I yearned to. And as long as he was near, I could never love anyone else.

"And then there was the Needle," Wolf continued. "The ingenuous way to separate his death, to take it away from his body so that he could enjoy his life without aging or fear. Again, you were the perfect guardian for it, Marya. Your powers, your solitude, your devotion, made the Needle safer with you than it could have possibly been with Kashchey himself."

"Why can't you just leave us alone, Wolf?" Kashchey asked. "What went between me and Marya is none of your business. Why go through all this trouble to destroy our Solstice night? Why do you care?"

Wolf turned to him. His eyes gleamed with an expression I read as triumph. But I also caught more in their depths. Bitterness. Pain.

"You know this feeling, Kashchey? Of deeds long past, coming back to bite you in the face?"

"What do you mean?" My father's voice faltered. He was afraid, I realized. Afraid beyond measure.

"Elena was my ward. I swore an oath to keep her safe."

The silence that followed was filled with the echoes of deeds long past. When I could no longer bear it, I fought for strength to turn to Kashchey and meet his dark gaze.

"Why, father?" I whispered. "Why did you have to kill Elena?"

Raven's eyes opened in a flash.

"You killed her, Kashchey?" The air trembled from the power in his voice. "*You killed her?*"

He was faster than anything I'd ever seen. Faster than the Gray Wolf himself, and much faster than Kashchey could ever be. He darted down from the branch and stripped the Needle from Wolf's mouth. Rising high into the air, he bit it with his deadly sharp beak.

A snap echoed loudly over the water. The Needle broke, its pieces dropping in a terrifyingly slow motion, straight into the whirling waters of the Sacrifice Pool.

The ground shook with thunder. My father, Kashchey, as if struck by lightning, began to twist into impossible shapes as he burned from within, with a cold fire visible only through his eyes. His face contorted in agony, morphing his dark, handsome shape, into an old, gnarled one, and then on to a distorted corpse, and worse, an inhuman monster.

I couldn't draw my eyes away from the horror I knew I would never forget, no matter how hard I tried. His screams seemed to go on forever. They still echoed after his body finally crumbled into pieces, and then into dust.

And then a wind blew, carrying away what was left of my father, my entire life, my world...

I woke to the feeling of someone's hand gently stroking my cheek, someone holding me in his arms and supporting my lifeless body.

I was blind and unfeeling.

I was dead.

I was a bird that flies above love, forever out of reach.

I was a dove, the daughter of a prophetic Raven and the beautiful maiden who betrayed him, and was betrayed in turn.

I was the Mistress of Kupalo, and I could never feel.

197

A voice whispered in my ear, like the whispering of grass in the fields of wheat and cornflowers on a bright summer afternoon.

It was that voice that made me slowly remember my body, limp against the lively form that supported it and kept it from collapsing on the ground.

It was that voice that made my senses slowly return, one by one, so that I could feel the chilly morning breeze on my face and hear the rustling of leaves and the soft murmur of the flowing water.

I still couldn't see, but I realized then that my eyes were shut, that they were closed forever, that I was unable to bear the loss of my father, my world, the man who made my weaning into new life feel like death.

"Marya," the whispering voice called to me, and it was not my father's voice that said it, it was not my father's hands that caressed me, taking away my pain.

I was alive, I realized. I actually existed.

Ivan spoke. I heard his words as if from a great distance.

"Marya, it's all right now. You're free."

He was talking to me.

Free. How could I ever be free from the horror I just witnessed, from the emptiness it left behind? How could I ever be free from the deeds of my past? I had been used and taken advantage of by the man who was my whole world, by the man I believed to be my father. He had forced me to do despicable things. And now, he was gone. Forever.

"Marya," Ivan said.

I clung to him, inhaling his natural scent of freshness and sunlight. Tears streamed down my cheeks and I felt his hand gently wipe them away. He held me to his chest and I buried my face in it, shaking with sobs.

He stroked my hair, words flowing over my limp form in his arms. "I know this is not the time to talk about such things, but I just wanted you to know. Ritual or not, I didn't—didn't mean to force you to marry me. You don't have to. I will never do anything to hurt you again. And—I'm sorry. I truly am. I never wanted to bring you pain."

Part of me understood the words. The other part wanted nothing more than to be soothed by the sound of his voice, his caressing hands, his arms cradling me as if I were a child. I heard his words, but my mind couldn't follow them.

There would be time for this later, to think, to decide, to regret. Perhaps there would be time to get to know him better, this boy of age-long wisdom who cut his way into my heart like a spring sunbeam cuts its way through winter ice.

Free. I am free.

I opened my eyes.

The new day was dawning. Alyona was gone, but the rest of the participants were all present.

Except Kashchey.

The Gray Wolf sat at the very edge of the water, the halo of rising sun shining at his back. He watched us with an expression I hadn't yet learned to read. Raven sat beside him. Sunlight bathed his feathers, making him gleam as if covered with molten gold. I couldn't make out the expression on his face at all.

"Father."

"Marya," Raven said gently.

"I—"

"You are free now," he said. "And I hope, from now on, you will be happy."

I nodded, feeling the warmth spread through me at his gentle expression. And then, I turned my head to look at Ivan. The warmth of his smile washed over me and I felt as if coming home, as if a part of me that had been missing for the longest time had finally found its way back to its rightful place.

I belonged here, in his arms, I realized. And it was all up to me now. I did not have to leave him again. If I wanted to, I could be with him for as long as we both lived.

For the first time in my life I felt complete.

Like the yellow flowers of the small forest plant, I'd found my way into the shelter of the purple leaves, which together make a complete living thing, a single inflorescence. *Ivan-and-Marya.*

ACKNOWLEDGEMENTS

This book roots in some very personal experiences in my life, and it took many years to bring it to its present state. I have so many people to thank for the inspiration, as well as for working with me on bringing this book to completion. First of all, my high school teacher, Galina A. Sokolova, for introducing me to the Russian tradition of the Solstice celebration. My family and friends, for sharing my fascination with the Russian folklore and for patiently reading earlier versions of this book. Members of the Online Writing Workshop for Science Fiction, Fantasy, and Horror, especially Rhonda Garcia, Clover Autrey, Mike Blumer, John Borneman, and Larry West, who were so great in spotting the gaps in the story and encouraging me to flesh out the essential details.

Last but not least, I thank my editor, Edwina Harvey, for bringing in the final touches that clicked everything into place.

ABOUT THE AUTHOR

Anna Kashina grew up in Russia and moved to the United States in 1994. She has a Ph. D. in molecular biology and is a published author of fantasy and historical fiction in Russia, Germany, and the United States. She lives in Philadelphia, Pennsylvania, where she combines her successful career as a scientist and her passion for writing.

Discover other books by this author by visiting Anna Kashina's web page (www.annakashina.com).

More from Dragonwell Publishing:

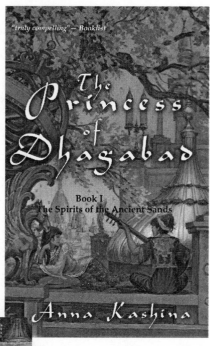

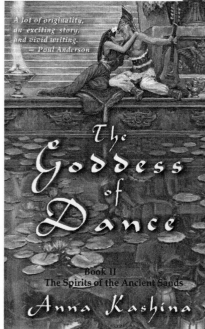

www.dragonwellpublishing.com

More from Dragonwell Publishing:

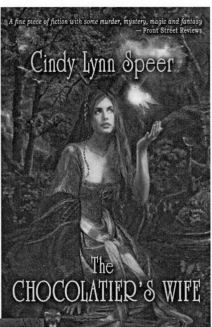

CPSIA information can be obtained at www.ICGtesting.com
Printed in the USA
BVOW03s2042051113

335549BV00002B/3/P